A SEASON

of

FIRE & ICE

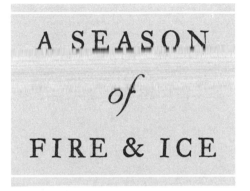

A SEASON

of

FIRE & ICE

*Excerpts from the
Patriarch's Dakota Journal,
with Addenda*

LLOYD ZIMPEL

UNBRIDLED

BOOKS

Unbridled Books
Denver, Colorado

Library of Congress Cataloging-in-Publication Data

Zimpel, Lloyd.
A season of fire & ice : excerpts from the patriarch's Dakota journal,
with addenda / Lloyd Zimpel.
p.   cm.
ISBN 1-932961-19-4 (alk. paper)
1. Frontier and pioneer life—Fiction. 2. Dakota Territory—Fiction.
3. Diary fiction. I. Title: Season of fire and ice. II. Title.
PS3576.I515S43 2006
813'.6—dc22
2005035593

3   5   7   9   10   8   6   4   2

Book design by SH • CV

First Printing

To Virginia

ACKNOWLEDGMENTS

Parts of this book first appeared, often in different form, in
the following magazines:

*Alaska Quarterly Review, Arkansas Review/Kansas Quarterly,
Missouri Review, North Dakota Quarterly, Sou'wester, South Dakota
Review,* and *Whetstone*

With thanks to E.V. Griffith, Diana Rathbone, and Greg
Michalson

CONTENTS

Beidermann's
First Year

1882

MAR. 19. Before first light comes the honk of geese above, but we are not misled to believe they portend an early thaw. While the winds warm somewhat, the river stands solid. Hay is adequate still, though lacking some quality, in that it is the last cutting.

A new homesteader, by name Beidermann, has settled to the south. Otto, going to the river and beyond to see to the new calves, brings back this news, which is of some curiosity in that the newcomer is the first to claim in that southern region which slopes into the valley, the last good sections before the bleak hills. Even more to our wonder, if as Otto attests it is true, the new man arrived at the New Year, those weeks being most severe, so that a man not well sheltered, as Otto says Beidermann is not still, could well have gone under in the blizzards and cold that descended then. The man Beidermann, with only two wolfish dogs, says Otto, camps in a draw, hard by a seepage of warm mineral waters, unknown these years to Otto or me or the other boys, though we have gone after deer and prairie hens near where it is. So this newcomer is a man upon whom God and fortune smile, or Otto would have come upon not him but the bones left by his dogs.

Ma vows to provide this man a welcome, that meaning a gift of her bread and a geranium, which she husbands through the winter freeze in every corner; although Otto is doubtful that Beidermann, who he found lacked congeniality in his disposition, will take pleasure in geraniums as decoration for his camp. But Ma has made her plans, that when the weather permits she will send the twins with welcoming gifts; for this man, as she says, is not only our newest neighbor, but now our nearest one.

APR. 12. This morning at the crossing I found trees down again, and have some urgency to clear them while ice remains, that we need not contend with the ugliness of flood and stranded stock.

The day staying fair, from the crossing I rode south and came in surprise upon the new homesteader Beidermann, with his dogs, which before any greeting passed between us, he had vigorously to whip back from my gelding, which in fright for good reason, unseated me, and I was left uninjured but mighty sore. My ready offer to shoot his animals then and there, the newcomer took in the spirit with which it was offered, and thus our early footing was an uneasy one. However, I put that aside, in part, and talked some, for we are nearest neighbors after all, and it was an occasion for sizing up by both parties.

This Beidermann is a large-boned man, but not fleshed out as are some with a similar frame, firm bodied and of more than medium stature, somewhat like myself as a younger man, for all that I lack such a generous and bent nose and eyes the color of split coal. He is, I have the understanding, without wife or family anywhere, although of an age when most men are long thus blessed or, as the sour Krupp says, burdened; and his undertaking of this enterprise is solitary, which I can see suits a disposition made plain in his behavior toward me and toward his savage curs.

Where I came upon him considerable timber is down along the bank, so he is occupied in getting together the means for his cabin, in the doing of which he gives no suggestion of wanting help. At one juncture he warns—he does not ask—that as the weather allows he will cross my land with his stock and goods, fetched down from where he does not say. From me he seeks no information, and I see in him a feeling that he, the newcomer, offers me, long settled, more than I offer him.

All the same, I put out some advice: to hold his dogs off my stock when he comes through. Looking at them and me with a near smile, he says, Yes, they are mean sons of bitches for certain.

APR. 21. Ma has thoughts of the solitary Beidermann, who, as she says, lacks a comforting bride and family, and with a twinkling eye asks if in my opinion Swede Jenssen's widow can smell a bachelor nearby; I say that it is my opinion that Beidermann having lived the winter in his close camp, then all Dakota can smell him. She speaks often of the Widow's well-being, whose husband went under two years past from injuries on our binder. For all that the Widow is a rail of a woman, ill-tempered to her girls and with flocks of geese whose clamor is heard in the next section, she keeps the Swede's homestead, as other widowed women would not keep that of their dead husbands, but flee.

Today the twins go by buggy to Beidermann's place, with a welcoming kit for him of bread and currant jelly, a small salt ham and a damned geranium. Beidermann having ignited no benign flame in my own breast, I am cool to the undertaking, the more so for my two youngest boys being gone dawn to dusk, although with a good horse, their rifles, and my warning of the wolfish dogs, and advice to hold to the river trail. Not least, they take their own good sense, this being deficient in none of my children, I may say, however they may sometimes misplace it.

Full of piss and vinegar they set off, to return long after supper, as we are ready to go out after them, enthusiastic at their adventure, having taken prize three shot rabbits, each lad claiming two, and no greater sport than having ventured a foolish, if successful, shortcut off the river.

Their news is difficult to believe, for they report that Beidermann has raised his cabin as well as beams for a shed; and his stock, which includes a fine team of Percherons, is on hand, in some way spirited along the river without my knowledge or that of Otto or any of the boys, for all that it is the only way in. As he warned me he would, he did, and leaves a puzzle as to how.

The twins report that Beidermann, confounded by the geranium, was yet civil at the gift of provisions; and fed and watered their horse, with which he showed a horseman's hand; and provided jerky for them, which bore green spots, although Beidermann himself ate it heartily.

His beef stock is numerous, say the twins, having seen a portion of it, and milkers as well, although it is a mystery to me how they feed, except that he has gone to Krupp or Myers for hay and fodder, for he has not come to me. In the bottom section of his land, say the twins, grass sprouts abundantly, and if this is so and it is already sufficient to feed his herds, it is nothing a man could rightly expect without the Almighty's magnanimous hand, and good fortune to boot.

If the twins report the truth, and not an overreckoning sprung from the inspiration they find in being alive on Earth in spring, then Beidermann is a man with gifts, and we need give him none. His plows and discs and harrows are oiled and gleaming, say the twins, so this aspect of his enterprise does not exceed my own, and perhaps the earth will not turn furrows in itself for him, as it does not for any man.

MAY 2. The twins come in triumph from a morning at the river, having captured three mallard hatchlings, which they would pen and feed as pets, for all my warning that these are creatures of the wild, with quirks of spirit that make them unaccepting of the lives of chickens; no sooner would the buffalo of these prairies yield to an oxen's yoke. But they protest it is a thing that Beidermann, whom they encounter always in their venturing, vows that he has done, this raising of wild ducks, and they would believe him first before their father, since he is a man of odd accomplishments.

So I hear much of Beidermann although I do not see him, past the single instance of my encounter with his ugly dogs—and these, say the twins, they find to be animals of good nature when circumstances are favorable, and ready hunters.

MAY 2J. The twins having persuaded Henry and Cornelius to take their Sunday chores, travel to Beidermann's place again, and he, for all his stony disposition, from their account willingly suffers the company of two boys hardly wet behind the ears, and does so to their advantage in learning ways of doing: as example his skinning of a heifer brought down by an unknown ailment; this unpleasant work accomplished by Beidermann driving a stake through the animal's head into the earth, and slitting the hide about the neck and down the belly, the neck-flap being hitched to his team, which then pulled it off, head to heels, in one swoop, as they report, like a man peeling off a tight mitten.

This Otto scoffs at, saying the hide would tear; but it is my recollection that this was done with buffalo one summer, by a band of drunken skinners, so it is cause to ponder whether it is in that company that our Beidermann learned his skill.

Returning today with horses worn down too much to please me, the twins tell of aiding our southern neighbor in the ambush of a coyote, this told with awe at the matching of Beidermann's wit with that of the prairie's wily nuisance; the deed achieved with the two of them proceeding in a long circle-round that drove the beast to reveal himself for one instant within the range of Beidermann's Winchester; while the twins, acting in faith on Beidermann's direction, saw never a hair of the animal until, hearing the weapon's distant report, they rode down gully and over hill to find the animal expired at Beidermann's feet. As reward for their good effort they have the unsightly tail, and although weary, squabble for its possession, which Ma requires they leave outside.

Otto and Cornelius and Henry mistrust their account, that Beidermann is so surpassing clever, having themselves seen samples of the coyote's guile; and the boys, being green, easily fooled. But Ma is admiring of the man for the way the twins look up to him, and for his *lessons,* as she says, to them; although in my opinion the degree of their admiration is excessive.

AUG. 2. By roundabout return from Krupp's place, I run up upon Beidermann this day as he comes from a draw east of the river, myself not eager to lay eyes on him by reason of my mood of gloom after a few hours in the bleak company of Krupp, having traveled to his place to help him plan out needed ditching, his yard being underwater every spring, and Krupp himself, in my opinion, inept at any matter requiring the exercise of logical thought, which I provide as a neighborly duty; thus subject to his dark talk of *drouth,* as he will call it, although himself never victim to the deadly parch long past, when stock fell thin as the branches of the scrub they chewed for the bark and stuck bellowing in the river's mud, and kernels of wheat at their fullest the size of mites, hard as stone. We have dryness, true, but Krupp has lost no stock nor will he; wheat and corn do not flourish fully, yet they survive and promise a yield not so meager that any will suffer; for the Lord provides sufficiently, and if not always in such munificence to allow His charges to accumulate a profit they do not need and which, in their possession, does lead to pride and vanity and a corruption of the spirit as afflicts Krupp, who looks for easy riches as they issue from harvests brought forth with little thought or effort.

Upon such thinking I am impelled to travel homeward in a roundabout way, that I may pass over the neighboring portion of Beidermann's land, as if there I might see such evidence as Krupp's *drouth* has laid upon it, with no plan to see its owner, who comes in sight suddenly, and I cannot turn my back, so ride to him.

His Percherons draw a hewed-log stoneboat with fieldstones collected from the dead furrows where he has rolled them out of his plow's way, these for the foundation of his new barn, he informs me, the roof of which he vows to raise before first snow flies. His dogs come from the hollow from some unholy hunt, and Beidermann warns them away.

He stands spread of leg atop his pitching load, pipe in teeth like captain of a ship. Coming in sight of his place I see how far he has taken the preparation of his barn, this revealed in the pile of shaven poles and rough sawn boards and the extent of the dug footings. This is admirable and I so say, at which juncture he puts in that he would find useful the help of the twins, saying this abruptly, as if by now they are naturally his to use and I have been unjustly withholding their labor from him. Then I have cause to feel that it would not be unneighborly of me, as it would be to another, to deny him their help, for reason of his incivility in asking it: such brisk demand will raise the back of any man. Yet I swallow his manner, and now the twins will turn their hand to Beidermann's carpentry.

Departing, my view is of the well filled with deep and clear water, over which stands a pole frame supporting blades that spin silently in the wind; so there is Krupp's *drouth* for Beidermann.

. . .

SEPTEM. 19. I observe that every fall seems meaner than the last in some way; in this particular instance by reason of the labor not lessening although the fruit thereof does lessen. Now Krupp, Hansen, Schneider and the Welshman Karn are all threshed out, and no crop fully satisfying but for Beidermann's, completed the day past, this being his first year's crop; and I and Schneider and others stand as the first of it comes in, the twins atop two racks, one drawn by Beidermann's team and the other by my sorrel geldings; more boys following with racks pulled by their fathers' teams; and all of us watch in silence this parade of plenty that we have seen from our own fields in years past but not this; as if what has failed to come to us has gone to Beidermann in the boundless good fortune the Almighty grants him, and I am caused to wonder what touch it is that serves him abundance and others only sufficiency, but make no complaint, even in my own mind, for what is sufficient is indeed enough.

In his feeding of the crew, Beidermann puts trust in Ma, who offers its organization, fearing that in his bachelor ignorance he will forego altogether his duty in this regard; and taking Swede Jenssen's widow as associate, that Beidermann might get himself a close look at her charms, which, in my opinion, do not exist, and a few other wives and daughters, Ma fills the long table under the boxelders with the vittles our host provides. These are not the beef and corn and beans familiar at other tables, but here squirrel, the number of which amazes Ma, saying as she does that he has surely depopulated all nearby standing timber of these little creatures, for the quantity he skinned, with the twins helping, causing me to ask of them whether Beidermann employs the singular method of removing squirrel hides as he uses on his dead heifers. With snap beans and cabbage, he supplies as well a pickle-looking squash, and this being new to the women, defeats them in its cooking, so that it is served up as a runny mush that Schneider's hired man crudely puts a name to as what he had shoveled from the pen of a sick calf yesterday. All of Ma's baked bread is soon consumed, that being familiar. There are looks around the table, but no grumbling; and I take it that the others' thinking is as my own: Beidermann has different ways which do for him, but they may not serve others well.

The crop in, and before leaving, I become more than a little acquainted with Beidermann's barn, the twins prevailing upon me, and their older brothers as well, to inspect every foot of it, that they make take pride in their contributions, these being many, from shingling to the straw chinking to hanging doors, so they say. It is a handsome structure of considerable dimension in which Beidermann will winter many head of stock; more, I calculate, than we are able; and with water piped to it, not only to a stock tank built of stones and mortar—this too bearing the mark of the twins' hand—but to a pump inside, the twins reporting that water runs to his house as well, but that I have not seen, having not been invited inside to see that or any of the furnishings of Beidermann's life, such observations made only by the twins, who show me now their power to command Beidermann's savage hounds to back away and behave.

In the buggy traveling home Ma says: A nice woman would do him good.

Then he will have to send for her, I say, although I know it is the

Widow Jenssen she means, but for the stony Beidermann to court this snippy, shrill-voiced woman with her houseful of girls as noisy as her flocks of geese brings up a picture my mind cannot take in.

He showed courtesy to her at dinner, Ma says.

⊸ *1883* ⊶

JAN. I. On the first day of the New Year, with the sun on the drifts bright enough to blind, comes Beidermann on snowshoes, his first time to our place, and at Ma's urging sits to coffee and Christmas cake with us all, but doing so uneasily, as would a man unused to woman's company in a warm kitchen. Nor are we easy with him, in that he comes as a surprise, although the twins do show such satisfaction in his company that he hauls up a stiff cordiality and offers me, and Otto as well, his plug to cut for our pipes, and we are soon all smoking together, at which juncture Beidermann reveals his purpose.

These little boys of yours are damned fine workers, says he, which causes the twins' ears to redden.

That is the way I have raised them up, say I, but without appreciation for his profane speech.

This is the New Year, says Beidermann to nods all around, and today we enter a new season. I am a man who sets straight his obligations of each year past before he embarks upon yet another, and it is my practice at this time to settle square with one and all.

Here he withdraws from the straw in his sack two small objects, and beckoning the twins forward, presents them each with one.

Ma and the boys and I draw close to see what gifts these are, to find they are blown goose eggs, every spot of each covered by a fine and delicate rendering in tiny painted strokes of a pastoral scene of a storyland country, not unlike the etchings in my books from London, although not in black ink but in the brightest of colors. A tiny shepherd and his tiny flock on the banks of a blue river encircle one egg, and the other bears the depiction of a farmer and his little girl at their cottage door overlooking a green meadow beneath the arch of a brilliant rainbow; on both the strokes appear done by a single hair of the brush, and with the touch of a fairy.

As they come to my hand for examination I hold them high for Ma to see, but her excitement is provoked not by admiration for Beidermann's artistry, but for another reason, in that she whispers to me, somewhat loud, Those are eggs from Anna Jenssen's geese!

So that is the end of Beidermann's first year, and now we go on.

Beidermann at the Flood

1884

APR. 18. All are asleep now. The room smells of swamp mud from our boots and britches, and from my dank hair. I am too much worn and the hour too advanced to recite the dismal business that has occupied my boys and me these two days past, other than that I will put a name to our fear, which amongst ourselves we show reluctance to do. But now it must be counted certain, yes, that Beidermann is lost, for there is no portion of the flooded wilderness as lends itself to penetration where we have not already gone; and if we cannot go in, then unlucky Beidermann cannot come out. He is lost, we must say so.

APR. 19. We must give up this looking, we must say to one another that Beidermann is in the hands of the Almighty, delivered there in the cruel way such as occurs in the blackest of dreams. There is no more we can do; I say so to Otto and Cornelius, and they, being the oldest, are of similar mind. Yet the twins are dauntless in their youthful hope—Beidermann *will* be found beyond the next muddy island of tangled brush and cottonwood snags. When the others of us ride home in weary silence, these confident two camp in the cold night mist above the flood, waiting for the dawn to renew their search; and from this I would not detain them, for such spirit, in their tender years, is deflected only at risk of injuring it forever, and that I have never done with any of my boys.

APR. 20. Otto and Cornelius stay home to their duties this day, attention to the stock being overdue; and while I thought to remain with them, instead, the milking over, I ride out with Harris who goes to Beidermann's place to feed the penned animals there, or they will starve; while I turn off in the cold wind toward the river. And so while I say I have no hope, I have some hope still; and in consequence tread the morass south of the fork, calling Beidermann's name; and hearing sometimes in the distance, above the loud slap and hiss of the water and hidden by islands of sodden willow or tangles of weed-caught brush, one of my boys calling the same. No reply comes; only the cry of the redwing blackbirds trying for perches on a patch of cat-tails soon flattened as the swift channel sends down a tumbling shape, perhaps one of Krupp's black bulls.

Under the light of this lamp, as the others sleep, I can sustain hope no longer, nor will it revive with the dawn, as it sometimes does. So too it is with Harris, confessing as we ride tiredly home in the dark, that futility seizes him. For all that he is the youngest next the twins, he has an old man's cynical misdoubts and few of their youthful expectations of eternal good and foresight of immortality. Perhaps the twins persist through simple affection for Beidermann, for all that he is not so likeable in the eyes of many. But he favors the two in his telling of fancy stories of water running uphill, and Indians riding the ghosts of buffalo through fierce blizzards; and commands their fascination at his rough-hewn ways of trapping wild duck live, and skinning ground squirrel with one yank of his hooked finger. For all that their loyalty is to the man's peculiarities rather than to his strength, I still cannot disaffirm it, for that loyalty is learned at my own knee and that of their mother. But now their expectations must meet a grievous end, for our stubborn neighbor surely is gone under in the unforgiving waters: even the able Beidermann, so certain in his own sufficiency, cannot make his challenges with impunity forever.

APR. 21. This day, as the twins continue at the river, the others of us bend to our chores—for animals and land have no patience—although we do so with burdened hearts, our thoughts with Beidermann and his fate. Harris, going off to tend the lost man's stock, says, What call did he have to be out there, in it? And though I do not voice it to the youngster, I have the answer to his question.

It is five days past that I saw Beidermann; I see him astride his mare, his wolfish hounds attending, as I go to examine the mud fence on the southern bottoms, erected there to prohibit the range stock from the eroding cliff above the river, all this swept away now and lying under the unruly waters.

I say unruly, but they are more than that. Indeed, a horrendous turmoil of water, far, far more of it than I have seen in any of my years on these plains; and flushed upon us with such surprise that no neighbor had opportunity to forewarn another, none to foresee the trifling Sheyenne engorge itself to such stunning proportion, spread a mile from its negligible banks, laying waste the bottom lands to the near horizon, only by the grace of God limiting its devastation to a strip of my holdings, but overrunning more of Beidermann's, Krupp's, Jenssen's—I cannot tell how much more.

I see him coming in the distance, the sturdy Beidermann, as I ride parallel to my vanished fences and mount a rise that looks down through the mist upon the forbidding sight—furious brown water battering hummocks of nettles and briars and head-high reeds and matted willows; cottonwoods with half their height drowned; the whole composing a labyrinth of wild islands scattered in an agitated sea; impassable and deadly for all the tangles of roots and half-afloat snags, chunks of white ice bucketing through, and the sluiced-up bones of buffalo. I see, in a deceptive backwater, a drifting log languishing beneath the surface, suddenly snapped up by an offshoot of the cruel current to swirl half above the surface and slap down splashing, as if hurled by an unseen hand; then to drift again on a quiet eddy amongst swamped hazelnut bushes and blackberry vines.

Two more of my heifers are here; one with only her rump rearing from the mud, and the bloated other a few rods into the river's center, pressed against a hillock of brush by the water's fierceness and battered by logs and ice and tossing limbs; both these animals having escaped over my mud barriers collapsed by the winter snows which, since the New Year, fell in a relentlessness outmatched only by the spring rains which followed, with this result. How many head of my cattle have gone under in it, I do not know.

My gelding snorts at the approach of Beidermann's mare. Up he trots without greeting, points a thick thumb toward the heifer's rump. Yah, he says, I lost eight–ten head in that.

I encounter him in the flesh so seldom, though suffering frequently the twins' reports of his doings, that I am surprised to see him now; and surely I am unprepared for the look of him, for he is dressed in good clothes which, upon the rough Beidermann, never given to close attention in his dress, would look queer even in congenial circumstances; here in the gray damp above the demolishing water he sits astride his mare in smart britches and a gray wool shirt and similar vest and a thick black coat of frock length, as a railroad agent would wear, its tail fluttered by the wind. That Beidermann should own such finery, let alone display it upon himself in this cheerless scenery, is another measure of his singularity.

But his manner says nothing of this, as he recounts the ravage upon his land, which is greater than that upon mine. Glaring narrow-eyed at the sweep of water, he points to a huge log tossing past. Good timber going to waste, he says.

Now his guess is that the worst has passed, for he claims to discern a drop-off in the water. Yes, he is sure of it, he says, as if to convince himself. He can cross.

This last I hear with astonishment. Cross the flood? What would persuade him to such folly, to attempt to cross this sinister tide? But if I suspected the answer to this question beforehand, now I am certain of it, and I hold my tongue; for I know it is true, then, the rumor passed along, perhaps aggravated, by the meddling Krupp, with his skill at gossip and complaint, about Beidermann's doings; here confirmed by the smart clothes, the lunacy of a proposed crossing when the western bank for which he must aim is not even visible in the mist. Into this he would throw himself, his mare, his ugly dogs—well rid of them, I would say—all for the sake of the spindly Anna Jenssen! It is beyond imagining, as Krupp himself admits, with a wink adding, And those two sections Swede left her has nothing to do with it either, eh?

At my side Beidermann muses to himself more than addresses me. Yes, he will cross; it can be done a mile upstream at the stand of cottonwoods whose L-shape marks an angle in the riverbed now made straight by the flood; at that grove, he vows, it is somewhat shallow, and his mare will need swim little distance, it being mostly bog, soft and dangerous, true, but passable to a cautious man who knows its perils and moves swiftly.

At such delusion in this staunch man I can only marvel. So inflamed by the long-jawed widow has he become that a half-mile of deadly flood is as nothing. There is silliness in his plan too, for even if he prosecutes a crossing undrowned, what will be the condition of his sporting clothes, having done so? The Widow Jenssen will welcome him as a pillar of stinking mud. But he is besotted; appetite shines in his eyes, and nothing I can say will stay him—he is not a man to schedule his behavior on the alarm of others. The Jenssen woman has wrought a transformation in the Beidermann bone and sinew, who, once a sober hard working man, has become a suitor as reckless as a dog with turpentine on his ass.

And more than suitor, I fear, if we can believe the scandalous footnote to Krupp's rumor claiming that the impassioned Beidermann has too vigorously set forth his case with the Widow, and in consequence she has with startling haste plumped up, like one of her own noisy geese penned to fatten for Christmas. This slyly attested to by Otto, he being the last to see her since that Holiday, a glint in his eye as he awaits disapproval from me, who has delivered so many moral preachments to my boys; but I do not give it outwardly, for all that I am sorely disappointed to find the stable Beidermann thus hauled in, whether by the Widow's scarce charms or her legacy of two sections of good land—whichever it may be, I am not one to further gossip, even amongst my own close kin.

And yet we have had a hand in this sorry development, or at least Ma's innocent finger shows, by reason of her matchmaking between these two, they having met at Beidermann's first threshing, at which Ma and the Widow Jenssen set his table for the hands, he being a bachelor of such undomestic bent that they feared he would ignore the feeding of the crew. There, then, the cackling Jenssen woman set her cap, and with such dire success that, had Beidermann been a small degree more likeable, less set and certain of his differing ways, and with less enviable achievement on his homestead, then he might have gained my friendly ear and sympathetic advice as well. But he is a man who rubs everybody against the grain, in that he himself is highly capable and displays scorn toward anyone who is not.

At the flood's edge Beidermann reins his mare past me, his dogs furtively skirting my legs as they watch for a nip—and it is cause to wonder how these vicious beasts disport themselves with the Widow's flocks of geese while the lusty Beidermann conducts his visits. It is beyond easy imagining, as is everything about this Beidermann folly.

So I am the one to see him off, that he may satisfy himself as to the safety of the Widow and her land; and see his mare wade into the boggy fringe of the flood above the L-shaped stand of cottonwoods and disappear behind them, his dogs romping in mad excitement.

APR. 22. The twins persist, Harris reporting them gone far south beyond the point of Beidermann's crossing, and he must hunt an hour to deliver provisions to them and grain for their pinto ponies, the grass being meager there.

To Beidermann's place with Otto this morning, and it is as Otto reports, quiet as death in the stillness of abandonment; as he found it when he came with bags of seed owed Beidermann to find him gone—that being the warning to send us searching at the river, where he had surprised me in his fine clothes. An eerie place it is without the presence of the master, and a little chill grows on my heart. The spinning windmill sends forth haunted groans, as might the ghosts of buffalo in Beidermann's tales to the twins, and we hasten to our chores.

Throwing corn to Beidermann's hogs, Otto says, I would not be surprised if the Widow got herself in the family way, but I surely never put the two of them together.

Pretending innocence, he hopes to tease me into disparaging comment, but I refuse his bait and say only, Now you know. There are no miracles in that aspect of life.

No miracles, to be sure; but gloomy mystery enough, I think, with abundant cause to ponder the peculiar inequity of purpose that summons the robust Beidermann from his unknown past, endows him with vigor and craft to prove-up his spot of Earth handily and without complaint, lets him set his roots, take a full grip, make his claim certain—and then he is swept away in one instant like a thing of naught, as if for some unknowable reason this stalwart mortal must not receive man's fair span upon the Earth, but only one pinprick moment as the river rises, as never before, to take him.

Will the Jenssen woman tenderly lay him out then, when the twins bring in his remains? It is a bitter thought, and I have received too much in my life to harbor bitterness; as I have gone too long unjudged, now to judge others. I do not know the inner man of Beidermann, nor the inner woman of Anna Jenssen; and of this Ma reminded me last night.

When the silent tobacco-chewing Swede went under from injuries on our threshing rig, at his funeral I watched his wife in a new widow's tearing passion badger her bawling daughters from pew to graveside, so fiercely demanding propriety from them as to show no grief herself, if it was in her; and I had the coldness to think that poor Swede by God's will was at last freed from the misery of a whipped and prodded life, delivered from the work he did by moonlight so as to stay afield long after supper until his wife was abed, thus to suffer her only from the time he pulled off his boots to when he fell asleep, and not the whole evening through, which time, when younger, he took pleasure in his fiddle playing, and while that brought little joy to others, it deserved better than the cruel derision of his wife. There was evidence, said Krupp with his sly mouth, that the man often made his bed in the barn, preferring the company of calves to that of his wife.

For such slim pickings the shrewd Beidermann wades to his death. Not even Ma will allow that the Widow is a catch—Ma with her generous measure of good-will and a pleasing word for the poorest of men or events, who once admitted, Anna ought to put some meat on her bones, which might give a lift to her disposition.

Well, say I, it is the meat on the bones that gives you your good nature, is it? For Ma is of that species of able cook unreluctant to be first at sampling the product of her own or any woman's Dutch oven. But Anna Jenssen is far from that, and the unhappy Swede, when he lived, was no more than a rail himself, lacking half his teeth, for all that his toothy wife seemingly possessed enough for them both, and raw-boned as a wintering steer, as if his wife's cooking, if he ate it, lent no subsidy to his body.

And yet, in human matters, there is always more. With all the snippy nature of her demeanor, the sniffish looks down her nose for no clear reason, the cackling laugh that tweaks the nerves, yet when the Swede went under and she was in the natural despair attending such circumstances, left alone with two young girls, with the lonely burden of keeping the Swede's homestead above water with the help of a procession of sorry drunken hired hands, not one of the afflicted lot staying out a season, so that Ma feared for her continuing soundness of mind—yet for all these encumbrances on her stooped shoulders, the Widow does persevere; and whether she does so by virtue of a strength carried unrevealed and secret in herself, or through blindness to the dire nature of her plight, which, clearly seen, would send her skirts aflying back East, as go others, still she endures. So it may be that Beidermann sees not a skinny woman, spare-legged and bent in the shoulder with a frizz of white Swedish hair on her lip like a young boy, but instead a rock of purpose, as stubborn as himself, here to stay. If that is what he sees, then the Swede's bequeathed homestead is only sugar sprinkled on the fresh bread.

WE THROW DOWN HAY for Beidermann's restive Percherons and swarming calves. Skittish hens importune us for more corn; the battle-ax blades of the windmill make their mournful moan, which is soaked up by the overlying silence.

If he has family, no one knows of them, says Otto. Who will take this over?

We are his neighbors, say I. It lies with us.

So we add to our own chores those of Beidermann, which one of the boys will go to do early each day until we are certain—until the twins have seen the certainty—that the hunt is unavailing.

APR. 23. From the twins, still on the river, comes no word; but for all their youthful daring, I know them to be lads of sense and ability, although Ma does fret—they are her babies still—and to put her worrying mind at ease, nothing will do but that I take them the bundle she has put up; and so I do, the day being young enough to travel to them and return by dark, which I have now done, and with heartening outcome.

When I reach the river the wet grass at the flood's edge still shows a rim of white frost from the freezing night, as if the Almighty has sketched a border around His watery handiwork. Of the twins or their hobbled ponies there is no sign as I ride south above the boiling water, here black with washed-away soil not soon to be replenished. As heavy a sight as I have laid eyes on, such ruination visited upon good men—how to be understood? Excepting we admit to the Almighty's Grand Design, wherein is inscribed our destinies, our fates, and Beidermann's doom.

Over the boggy ground, my gelding pulls toward firmer footing upslope, away from the splashing waters. The cold air holds the smell of fresh damp earth, underlaid by the rotting stench of varmints trapped and drowned: their cadavers toss swiftly past; jackrabbits, squirrel, a fox, the mangled furry mass of a prairie wolf, not so wily as to outwit the flood.

Somewhere here too, the remains of the incautious Beidermann, which the twins will come upon: not the first dead man they have seen, nor the last—for they bid to see me go, and Ma, and surely some of their older brothers. But Beidermann, long in the water, banged and buffeted by his passage through brush and snags and rocks, will be one they see more than once in their blackest dreams.

At that same L-shaped stand of cottonwoods where a week ago Beidermann prodded his mare into the soupy edges of the flood, here I draw up. A high hill of stripped roots and branches, flattened brush, half a privy, have anchored on a snag in the river here, an unwanted dam that will need grubbing out, perhaps timber to be salvaged, when the flood has had its say. If the water has pulled back since Beidermann challenged it, it is by inches only.

My gelding takes me up a little slope which offers a vantage to oversee the wreckage, and here, by chance of a narrow sight-line unobstructed by vine-tangled islands of bending willows, suddenly I have a view of unflooded land opposite, which is the dry western bank of the flood—a surprising prospect it is, perhaps a half-mile distant and fuzzed over by hanging mist, which sometimes clears for a moment as the wind veers.

In one such moment I glimpse a sight which causes my heart to quicken, for there is movement on that dry shore, on the slope far opposite, and I quit the saddle to get a steady view, and stare unblinking until my eyes are aching. It could be no more than a stranded animal, one of Krupp's bulls, or specters the imagination conjures.

But several figures stir there. It could be Krupp himself, it could be Gaustad from far upriver, seeking lost stock, or the incautious Widow Jenssen out in her buggy, doing the same. . . . Now the mist unfolds sufficiently to reveal three figures moving back and forth upon the shore. So fixedly do I stare that they blur into the mist, and I must close my eyes to rest them; it is as if the image is etched on the balls of my eyes, and too clear to misperceive. Indeed it is three figures I see, three mounted men and not ghosts; three men, one larger and two smaller, the smaller ones on horses of lesser proportion and lighter shade than the one— perhaps pintos. Moving along the shore they gain an elevation that limns them against the milky western sky, as in a lantern show. If the dogs are there I cannot see them, but there is reason enough to believe it is the twins and Beidermann.

I am surprised, and not surprised. How have the twins made this perilous crossing? It is a marvel; but the darker mystery lies with Beidermann, who survives. Yet I think not such a mystery, for this is Beidermann. Have the twins found him, or has he found the twins? It is enough that they are all safe—and yet they are not safe, for they must cross back; and whatever way the three have been spirited across the flood, whether borne—shall I fancy?—on the wings of Beidermann's goatish passion, that way must be rediscovered for their return. If it is a lesson needed to be learned, then Beidermann has taught it.

I see my stout neighbor venture into the flood to his mare's withers, the twins' ponies skittishly following. A thin rain commences, obscuring their dodging progression, hummock to hummock, across the water; but I feel easy they will soon be on the bank where I stand.

So I now await them at home, where Ma fries ham and potatoes for the twins' supper, and asks if she might lay a plate in expectation of Beidermann; but I tell her, No, for he is sure to go his own way. . . .

On his way with his team to borrow old man Praeger's hayrake, the bachelor Beidermann got to thinking, as he often did these days, about the Widow. He rode first along the slim and sometimes disappearing trickle of the Sheyenne, then turned up the slow rise north, his dogs far ahead, barking now and then at an antelope or a rabbit, or an imaginary one. He would be all forenoon getting there, and he was soon in serious consideration of the Widow, having quickly dismissed the image of her as last seen a week earlier, chasing her geese out of the squash, it being a toss-up which was the noisiest, the geese or the Widow Jenssen.

He figured her for north of forty, beating him by a good half-dozen years. She looked it, too: thin, stooped, hard-skinned. Her girls were eight and ten, meaning she'd married late, probably delighted to find herself married at all at that age. Swede Jenssen, he knew from remarks old Praeger kept making—as if this was something he'd never forget—had passed away from injuries caused by Praeger's binder rolling over him. Now three years dead, Swede had been a man of singular quality, if the windy old Praeger could be believed, although no youngster. Some old geezer, maybe, whom Anna had finagled to the altar. A good worker, though; you could tell from the shape his place was still in; even the old sod stable was still standing. He had left a nice piece of land. . . . And that was a thorny matter too, for any interest Beidermann took in the Widow might look to some like interest in the two sections she had managed to work by herself now for seven years, with the help of whatever drunken hand hung on for a month or two before she had to fire him. . . . Well, people could think what they wanted, but there was nobody who'd say anything to his face.

For that matter, Beidermann wondered if anyone had even pegged him as courting the Widow. It wasn't clear to him that he was. Probably he was, since he called on her for no purpose, and it was a long haul to her place, no closer than to Praeger's. But he hadn't given her any real presents . . . those deer steaks, and he had done most of her butchering last fall. . . . In the spring she had given him a half-dozen goose eggs to put under one of his setting hens, but they'd turned out to be infertile, so he'd blown out the dried contents, painted the shells for ornaments, and returned them, to her astonishment.

So perhaps he was courting . . . but it was nothing like the business with that girl years before up in Buford. Of course, he was only twenty-one then; she was fourteen. She wouldn't come down to Bismarck with him—so his courting couldn't have been that successful—even though her pa all but hit her in the head to make her go. She wouldn't do it, though. . . . She was something: long black hair like an Indian's, but shiny clean; soft, bright cheeks. . . . Whatever might have happened to her? A grown woman now, probably with a daughter or two herself. He hoped she had gotten as far away from that bastard old man of hers as he had from his.

HE WAS ASTRIDE the mare's broad back, a moth-eaten buffalo robe doubled over to give some cushion against her iron backbone and the harness hip-strap. The team held to a shambling trot, harness jangling. In these lower parts there was dampness enough to keep the ground a little spongy, the grass slightly green, and the air breathable. His cattle were somewhere along here, to the south, he figured; he had seen neither them nor old Praeger's, but there was plenty of sign in the dried mud.

Now, coming out of the bottom, the mare and her gelding partner slowed to a walk as they faced into the drouth's heat. . . .

"Drouth? Drouth?" old man Praeger had scoffed. This was just one more dry spell. "You haven't seen drouth," he told Beidermann.

"This'll do me," Beidermann said.

The thin line of cottonwoods that marked the outer rim of the river's flood plain offered a little shade; it dappled the horses as they trod under the trees. The two hounds had pulled in, too, at the heat, and instead of coursing ahead, noses high and yellow eyes seeking anything worth a chase, they trailed in the team's dust, tongues hanging.

. . .

LOOKED AT A CERTAIN WAY, Beidermann supposed, the Widow could be considered a catch, her years and Methodist ways notwithstanding. More than once, old Praeger's wife had let on that Anna was the prize heifer in these parts; until once Beidermann worked in a slick question, saying, that if that is so, how is it that none of this herd of overgrown boys running around your place have snapped her up; Otto, for one, being practically her age? That set the old lady to rolling her sharp eyes and furiously slicing up her raisin pie and pouring coffee like hell wouldn't have it. And all the while she was probably wondering the same thing: how to get a few of those big eaters—two were still little, the twins—away from her table and bellied up to some other woman's. . . .

FOR SURE, THIS WAS a day no cooler than it had to be, the sun as hellish today as every day for the last month. Praeger's "dry spell" and then some. Sweat soaked his shirt collar, buttoned tight against the sun, and both horses frothed where the cheek pieces rubbed. He was heading onto old Praeger's land now; soon the path turned from a bordering green to overall dun, then to gray dust. The sky, relentlessly without clouds, was a thin blue, where the sun had not blurred it white. It struck Beidermann that he was leaving a fertile valley to travel onto a barren plain. . . . Not true, he knew, but in his mind was some biblical equivalent of such difference, and he sought to recall it:

In green pastures lived the blessed, and in blighted wilderness dwelt the corrupt.

Something like that. His mother had read it to him as they sat on the log outside their dugout—it would have been early morning or early evening, times when his father was sure not to be on hand.

She had two Bibles, his mother did, English and German, and read from either handily. When she died, he had just started reading back to her from both, so clever had been her teaching. He remembered her first lessons from Proverbs:

Where no oxen are, the crib is clean,
But much increase is by the strength of the ox.

It means, she told him, you must do the unpleasant work of cleaning the stable if you want your cattle to keep their health and work hard to bring in a crop.

It was a memory that had come back to him often, when he was working a bull train and staring through the dust at a dozen dumb oxens' asses.

THE BLOTCHED SHADE offered by the sparse and wind-tossed cottonwoods ended. The horses pulled onto the prairie toward old Praeger's. Before he left the last of the shade, Beidermann pulled up and swung off the mare to relieve his bowels. As he squatted, the brown grass rose well above his head. Blackflies thronged to his loins, and cottonwood fluff floated down and then, whipped by the wind, sailed swiftly away. Shivering their hides against the flies, the big horses chewed whatever buffalo grass they could work past their bits. On a spot where the grass was blown flat, the two hounds took their rest, their long legs stretched in front of them, eyes nearly closed, panting so loudly that Beidermann could hear them above the wind. From where he squatted, he cast about for a handful of leaves that weren't too dry and brittle.

Back on the mare again, with the hide redoubled under his sweaty rear, he set the team onto the faint track north. Only his own previous journeys marked this trail. No one else had reason to travel this way to old Praeger's. Krupp came from the north; the Swede, when he was alive—or now the Widow—though she hated to take her horses any distance—from the west; and old Reinhardt came in, cursing his mules every foot of the way, from the east. That trail from Reinhardt's was an old wagon road from Saint Paul, but Beidermann remembered when the freighters had abandoned that route for a smoother one, with more water on the way, through Fargo. He remembered well, because one of the first bull trains on that road cost him his best dog, father of the bitch plodding in the dust behind him right now. The feisty bugger had decided to chew out the hamstring of the nigh ox on a Slide Bros. freighter, and the wagon boss hammered him to death with a slab of strap iron. It was something! The boss was a slop-bucket Dutchman whose screeching English Beidermann could barely understand, although it was clear he expected payment for his stricken bull, the beast still in its yoke, dragging down its terrified mate, trying to pull its useless leg under itself, and all the while bellowing and tossing, strings of its saliva hitting everything in sight.

Beidermann, when it came his turn to yell, demanded payment for his dead dog, a sum he claimed the equal of any damned ox, and so there was a fight, Beidermann sustaining a broken little finger that healed crooked. The Dutchman backed off when Applewine ran out of his stable and poked a rifle in his face. . . . He missed that dog, name of Lord, for a long time.

Now the expanse of plain ahead revealed nothing but more of itself, mile after mile of grass waving flat and dodging up in the wind. No tree, house or animal anywhere. To Beidermann, aboard the big mare, it was a comfortable sight, out of something his mother might have read him from the Bible. In so many places where he had been it had looked like this. It was how the world was meant to look. He knew exactly what was up ahead: it would be just like this. Yes, the world was finite, but Beidermann had seen some of the places that were said to be the end of it—said so by ignorant people who looked at the horizon and said: There the world ends. Beidermann was not one of them.

IT WAS ALMOST NOON before he saw the hazy outline of old Praeger's new barn. He had some dry meat and a biscuit wrapped in his pocket, and he ate without stopping, so that when old lady Praeger pushed dinner on him, as she was sure to do, he could pat his belly and claim he'd already filled it. Well, sure, he'd sit down to a piece of pie. That old woman could sell pie to the devil. And he wouldn't turn down a cup of coffee. Now he found himself looking forward to both.

Here the dust the team kicked up was as gray as the hounds who followed in it. Here was drouth, no question, and the blight seemed to have picked where it would settle heaviest: while old man Praeger bragged about *real* drouths, one had sneaked up and settled flat on him. The sight surrounding Beidermann was inauspicious. Even the Widow's place, farther out of the river bottom than old Praeger's, was in better shape, with a touch of green still, wheat with a sizeable kernel, corn promising at least half a crop. Swede had made a fair claim when he had settled; Krupp, too, was in decent shape; Reinhardt as well. Praeger's "dry spell" was hitting Praeger hardest, and why was that?

Maybe he was being prodded from on high for his damned gluttony, Beidermann thought. One man did not deserve that much land. Beidermann didn't know how much it was, but all the grown boys had made full claims—homesteads, preemptions, tree claims—and bought up relinquishments all around. Krupp told a snide story of old man Praeger even trading a pair of mules and a wagon for a quarter-section from a Norwegian who'd gone bust.

Old Praeger ran it all as one—a damned kingdom, Beidermann thought; and given the reach of it, bad weather at one end did not mean the same at the other. He wondered whether parts of it that he had never seen flourished now, while other parts, such as this he crossed, withered; and old Praeger, averaging it all out, came up with his "dry spell."

It was probably Otto's claim he was on, Beidermann decided, since it was near the river, next to where the old man claimed first, and Otto being the oldest would have made the second-best claim, which this looked to be.

Otto—there was a strange case. Why was he still kicking around his old man's place when he couldn't hope to see it passed on to him? Oldest son be damned. There were a couple of mean ones in the brood—Harris, Cornelius—who wouldn't hold to any "oldest son" bullshit. There was sure to be a fierce battle when the old man died. Yet Otto hung on where another man would long ago have found a life of his own. Did anything about that, Beidermann wondered, involve the Widow? He didn't think so, but he had seen a few old boys jump through some hoops for lesser women.

AT TIMES THE TRAIL swerved off through the brittle grass into two parallel tracks, then swept back into a single one. From a little distance, and on the slight rise in the prairie, this gave the trail a scalloped look; it was like the hanging trim of the fancy table the Widow had in the room behind her kitchen, on which her Bible lay. Beidermann recognized this with surprise, but then the wind folded down the grass to hide the design.

This was not a wind that stopped. Sometimes it lessened at dawn, again at dusk, but it never failed to build itself back to a stiff blow. Nor did Beidermann ever stop noticing it, although it was nothing he would have thought to mention. He remembered it as being perhaps a little worse above the border. It was always a matter factored without thought into the day's business. If he needed to travel twenty miles into the wind, then by instinct he would go twenty-one, for the wind would bear him back that lost mile.

As pretty as this country was with all its grass, there were spots above the border prettier still. Beidermann remembered high ridges in the foothills, no grass there, only yellow rock off which the sun glinted and the wind skipped cold even in the middle of summer, never mind winter. Those were ridges he had gotten to know well, following his pa, Adolf, who ran traps among them and into the mountains, high as a man would want to go, to places where snow lay all summer, never melting a drop. Ermine didn't bother to change into their summer coats, and Adolf bragged that from secret places that he knew better than he knew his prayers, he could bring in white skins all year round. No one else would go, as it was too risky, too cold, too hidden, too far. Many a time Adolf had taken little Leo when he was nine, ten—the age of old Praeger's twins now, though it seemed to him he had been bigger and tougher.

He recalled it well enough, those icy days and forlorn nights, riding always a quarter-mile behind the old man, who never waited, sore in the worn and cracked saddle Pa had traded a jar of whiskey for to a Sheepeater Indian. Old Adolf had upward of a hundred traps out, and every time Leo dragged up through the snow to see what the old man had caught his pa had already removed his catch; the frozen martin or fox was stuffed into the big pouch of the pack mule to be skinned when they camped, and the trap already rebaited or pulled. Without a word Pa had swung his stiff right leg across the saddle—it stuck out too far to fit the stirrup—and headed up the trail, leaving young Leo to stare at the new set—if, indeed, there was anything to see; a stake, smoothed-over snow, a bent branch. And yet, laying eyes on these things often enough, Beidermann somehow learned the traps with the old man saying hardly a word, other than to swear at him for snagging a line or getting his pony hung up in shoulder-high snow. And while he did learn, it stayed in Beidermann's mind that he had never set a trap to fool a wolverine, which the old man had done more than once. He had shot one of the bastards in later years, but never trapped one.

About snares the old man taught Beidermann one good lesson. While the boy was fastening a wire loop to a stout willow limb along a frozen creek where snowshoe hares ran, he clumsily managed to set it off, and with his own wrist snubbed tight, the sprung branch pulled him to his toes. He yelled loud enough to be heard in Regina. From a half-mile up the trail, his old man rode back, swung slowly off his horse and, before freeing young Leo, gave him a snowy boot in the ass with his good leg.

This was one story Beidermann still told about his pa, when he told any; and when one noon he told it to the Widow she was startled and drew up, saying it was something *her* father would have done too, would you think it? He had slapped her hard just for accidentally locking herself in the root cellar when she was nine. It wasn't fair. When she was naughty, of course she expected to be slapped, and if she was bad enough, even whipped. Beidermann nodded knowingly. The Widow went on, but when it was *something not your fault*

They were sitting over pie and coffee at the scallop-edged table, and what they told each other then sometimes drifted back into Beidermann's head—the trapped girl, the snared boy.

. . . That was all *another time, another place.* The phrase came to Beidermann suddenly, seeming meaningful. He recalled it as something old Praeger had said to him: another time, another place—that time being Praeger's youth and the place the Wisconsin woods. A terrible time, a terrible place, as the old man told it, a dark world of men cutting off their own feet with slipped axes; the screams of horses dragged down a hill by logs too heavy to haul upward; widows with clutches of knee-high children come to retrieve the bones of Gustav or Dieter still buried in the snow beneath the pine he'd been felling; men shooting into their own heads in fits of drunken insanity, their families giving silent thanks that it had been done before they had smashed in the skulls of wife, children, in-laws, as they had vowed to do, as God was their witness.

No wonder the old man had given that over to set up in the West; it was happenstance alone that he did not set himself up so handsomely as he might, for all the length and breadth of his holdings. Perhaps it was too much time in the woods, but he was an indifferent judge of prairie land. The southern sections that he might have had, Beidermann now held. And where old Praeger kept tacking on acreage, it was always in the wrong direction; for it was a mile past Praeger's southernmost boundary, in the center of Beidermann's claim, where by the greatest good fortune and the grace of Almighty God a copious spring had spontaneously bubbled forth during Beidermann's first summer. It poured forth out of what had been a rocky draw, without grass, let alone a trace of moisture. Now its waters ran miles into Beidermann's fields; he was proud enough to believe that had Praeger settled there, no water would have appeared for him.

ALL SPORT WAS out of his hounds in this heat. They padded behind. Old Praeger's barn shaped up clearly through the prairie haze. His horses could use water. They moved at a decent pace, a little slowly. Animals that size weren't made to travel fast. Even so, they were a quick team. At threshing at Schneider's, he had

matched them in a pull of loaded racks against four other teams—
one of looming Missouri mules, taller than his Percherons, though
not so wide—to run ten rods from a dead start. They had finished
a half-rod ahead of the big mules.

Beidermann doubted that any man who looked on those
horses failed to admire them, and most did so aloud. Last summer
in Skiles, when he'd brought in a load of hay that Applewine at
the livery stables had contracted for, a white-haired old man
emerging from Schwantz's Mercantile had suddenly seen the team
across the road and drawn himself up to take them in, hoof to ear
and nose to tail; he had walked up to run his hands along the
mare's leg and rump until Beidermann warned him off, and then
he'd said, not to Beidermann but to a small fellow sagging at his
side, "I'd pay five hundred dollars cash money for that pair right
here and now." He reached into his shirt pocket as if to produce
that sum until his friend poked him and said, "Not till you pay me
four bits for them shots."

In fact, Beidermann had seen real money offered. When he
was leaving Canada, a lame old snuff-drizzler at the border, who
was running sheep, from the looks of the few in sight, and house-
keeping in a dugout with a lean-to sod roof out front for a
kitchen, and a sullen Indian in ragged blankets as a hand—this
dwarfish old boy pulled a buckskin sack from out his britches and,
to Beidermann's astonishment, spread out in his crimped hands
what he claimed was three hundred twenty dollars in hard gold
coin: his offer for the team. He held his rifle snug under one arm,
waiting for Beidermann's response.

"What the hell would you do with them?" asked Beidermann,
who'd had the pair less than a year himself. Looking around into

the hard wind, he saw nothing but the old man's dismal cave, a few dozen sheep that had chewed up all the buffalo grass in sight, and sheep shit piled a foot deep around the muddy watering hole scraped into the creek.

"Them's fine horses," the old boy said, with a glaze in his eye.

Beidermann knew the look. It came from penniless old men imagining themselves slapping harness on these behemoths, hitching them to a new two-bottom plow—when they owned neither halter nor hoe. Understandable to Beidermann that a man who spent his days trailing sorry sheep would go a little queer in the presence of animals so unlike any others in his daily life, even though they would eat him into the poorhouse in winter. He had noticed that the Widow, too, with no talent for animals—unless those raucous geese counted—even she eyed them with quiet speculation. It was the same look Beidermann fancied she some-times directed at him. That was good for a chuckle. Folks might think he was after her place, but what if it was her coveting his horses?

Covet, he thought; a word pulled out of the past, when his mother had read the Bible to him. Always attached to it was *thou shalt not.* . . . It came attached, as well, to some feelings of his own. He had in mind the Widow's pearls. He did admire them; no less, he thought, than that sheepman admired his team.

It was the strangeness of them. They were the first pearls he had ever seen. They were three in number, centered amongst a few glass beads on a wire-string necklace. With no occasion to be worn, the string lay wrapped in flannel in the top drawer of her cedar chest. These—the pearls and the chest—said the Widow, were what her mother and grandmother had left her. Her girls clamored often to have the string brought out for a treat, to put in turn around each thin neck, for looks in the mirror. And so Beidermann was privileged to handle them more than once. They were yellowed and of uneven medium size. Under his crusty fingertips they were velvety as his mare's nose, a promised moist smoothness within. . . .

In the blowing, shimmering, sun-struck phantasmagoria he rode through, he could see himself as owner of the pearls, and the crippled sheep-follower the owner of his team, the two of them stunned, not knowing what they had done or what they would do next.

HE CAME ON toward old Praeger's southernmost planting: corn. It looked like hell. What there was, cutworms had got at. The old man wouldn't get half enough for winter hog feed. Drouth did it every time. . . . Yet Beidermann had seen corn worse than this, up on the border, where there was more wind. First sun dried the crop up, wind blowed it down, nothing to cut; send the kids to pull the stalks for burning in the cookstove.

Beidermann
and God's Gift

1885

MAY 29. The lively wind of the past three days abating, welcome weather visits us today; as the good Thomas Nashe has it:

Cold doth not sting, the pretty birds do sing,
Cuckoo, jug-jug, pu-we, to-witta-woo!
Lambs frisk and play, the shepherd's pipes all day. . . .
Cuckoo &tc. . . .

Having thus provided for our earthly comfort, can it be the good Lord now deems our souls might benefit from another laudatory report of the deeds and high accomplishments of the peerless Beidermann? For at supper come the twins squeaking forth news of our bachelor neighbor's latest feat; and while Ma shoos the begrimed pair to the pump for a wash, with their sour brothers I await, no less sourly, their shrill account, no triviality withheld, of Beidermann striding like Jehovah across his driest acres—those high, tanned pastures near hailing distance of the badlands, this being as arid a location as we have in Dakota, in which water is scarcely known by name, let alone by sight, where the paltry spring rains race unavailing across an iron earth—here, where every sign points from such an event, here Beidermann has uncovered water.

Yes! It is true! cry the twins; and he has divined it himself: he summons it forth from the thick crust with nothing but a damned willow twig.

What? says Otto, who as the oldest has the responsibility to speak sense. Did you see it? Did you see the water running? Did you feel it? Did you have a drink of it?

Oh no! The twins are surprised by his reckless supposition. The water is deep underground; he has only found where it is; the digging it up remains to be done.

Huh, says Otto. That is the test, then, in digging it out. Tell me when you have a nice cupful of it, and it doesn't burn your tongue off.

But the twins have no ear for such caution: they describe their hero Beidermann treading the golden hip-high grasses of his upper plateau, where even so early in the season, dust claims the earth and crushed grass blows its powder in dusty puffs from beneath his boots as he plugs on with his forked willow branch. Over the second helping of fried pork and gravy-potatoes which Ma delivers to their plates, the twins' eyes shine at the glory of it. Now soon, Radke, the well-digger, comes from Skiles with his rig to set pipe, and will that be a sight!

The older boys quickly put away their grub, to escape this chatter.

Oh, it was something to see! Over the baked land, the towering Beidermann, wand held out at the level of his belly button—

I wonder that he has one, growls Harris; and as he rises from the table, roughly shoves back the bench, near dislodging August, sharing it. The two join Henry, leaving the kitchen to rinse the milk-pails, little mutters and half-laughs coming from them as they go.

Across the dry land, the mighty wand extended, the twins in his dusty wake . . . until . . . until . . . the wand beings to dip—

No, cries the other, it does not dip. It jumps, like a horse jerks a rein right out of your hand. A strong jerk. Yes, it pulled itself almost out of my hand when he let me grab it!

Beidermann permits them each to hold the magic wand, although with one hand only, his own grip being required to power it; and when one of the twins holds it alone, it is no more than a dead stick. Beidermann is the engine.

At last, the kitchen left to Ma and me, we exchange a look, and I wonder if I see in her glance what is perhaps also in the twins' look as they go to throw down hay for the morning: if Beidermann can do it, why not this idling husband and father, forever grousing over lack of rain? Beidermann does it, how about you? But what is unclear in their heads is that it is one thing to parade around with a piece of stick and say, Here is water; and it is quite another to sink pipe foot after foot, yard after yard, rod after rod, until the money runs out—or perhaps first, by God's grace, comes a sweep of brown liquid to make a goat retch.

I have watched these water-witches practice their craft, and with the best of them it is a chancy business. Old Krupp claims his wife has the talent, although she will only mumble, maybe yes, maybe no; his Gladys, a fleshy woman, who a few years ago I watched waddle sweatily in a skirt of heavy brown ticking, in her hand a peach branch—the best kind, winked old Krupp—her goiter trembling shiny with dampness as she tramped the weeds in the parched field a mile behind Schneider's barn, the sweating Krupp, anxious as Schneider that she make good, a few yards behind, muttering encouragements or threats, one; but neither of benefit as the peach rod failed to detect even an armpit's moisture: and I remarked to the cast-down Schneider that he could as well follow Krupp's ornery mule and at the spot it takes its first dump, there call in Radke. . . . But it was later said that Gladys and her peach twig succeeded a time or two north of here, though I cannot attest to any truth in that.

JUNE I. They are off to aid in the digging, are the twins, saying Beidermann tells them to request my allowing their help; and given their admiration for our singular neighbor and his pursuits, which in general I do not share, to refuse such permission is to gain a brace of small enemies at my own table. Still, it is a factor in how young boys find their own ways to shape the lives ahead of them, that they have the chance to watch inventive energies at work, however queerly they are expressed; when else they would be at the drab business of following the dependable and far-from-eccentric Otto—and though saying this I bite my tongue, having given so much over to that fine boy that without his dependability we would all flounder.

So long as you do your chores, I tell them every time they ask; and these they do, even after the hard two-hour ride home: throwing down hay, washing the separator by lantern light. Weary as they are at supper, by dawn they pop up refreshed. . . . And in a week, we must realize, Radke the digger comes, and with his clever rig set into the shaft the lads with Beidermann have dug, will sink his pipe at fifty cents each foot. This they must see. And why not? For already they may well cast a proprietary eye upon all Beidermann's water, in that they have taken a hand in bringing in nearly every pailful that flows off his homestead.

JUNE 5. But is a single well enough for Beidermann, in whose head the spectre of drouth crouches like one of Satan's imps? There is the water in the river, which has supplied what he has got by on in these last years; but now he will have more: he vows to the twins, who help him here too, that no head of his stock shall ever want for a drink; and with the twins assisting, he gouges a new canal to bring still more of the river to him. They lead his team—the massive Percherons—a treat for the boys, no work at all to play master to these handsome animals, for they are horses of a variety a boy seldom sees, nor do many men; the shining behemoths nosing the tops of the boys' hats as they pull to Beidermann's shouted directions, the water-seeker himself heaving the scraper—I lent it to him—through sandy soil, rocky soil, and finally mud; thus bringing to ditch a hundred acres of his bottom land, where water was already, but now he has more, and artfully channeled.

And if one well is insufficient to our gluttonous neighbor, surely a single canal is not enough; and the twins follow Beidermann high up the river, past the last edges of Krupp's place, where grew—it grows no more—the last good timber axed down by Beidermann, then floated two miles downriver, there to be dragged up the sandy banks with a one-horse hitch, a twin to each horse, snaked there from over Beidermann's north acres where they border my own, and on to his place; whipsawed there into boards for a flue—the likes of which I have not seen here, although they are familiar in the Wisconsin woods, but for a different use. This one by Beidermann, I will say, is ingeniously devised, as it somehow teases water off the river's high bend at the loopy ox-bow where it last touches my northern range; and then by help of a funnel arrangement made of rocks, that portion of the river Beidermann makes his own, pours into the leaking zig-zagging pig-troughs he and the twins have pegged together, over a small bluff into a draw and then, by God, seeming to defy gravity, out of it; finding home at last in an ancient buffalo wallow, fried by the sun to hold water, which it promises to do until mid-summer.

Traveling up there a few days ago—where Beidermann has some fat heifers—and if he needs a few dollars for his well, I would take one or two of those animals at the right price—I see that my own cattle have learned the location of Beidermann's water: so far there comes no friendly complaint of trespass from him, nor should it, the junior members of my family having given such a substantial hand in the raising of that installation.

. . .

JUNE 6. Again, the lads are off at dawn, hastening to catch another day of Radke's profane efforts. Refraining from use of his language, they describe Radke addressing a crimped pipe, and as I know Radke, I fill in the words in my head.

They are at their hasty breakfast, and I seek the last of the coffee from the swimming grounds in the pot, and Harris, leaving the kitchen, calls back: Why do you let those boys help that lazy bastard all the time? Let him dig his own wells, like everyone else does. When you dug that well—and he points out the door at ours—did you get Schneider's little children to haul away the dirt?

He points across the table to the twins half-standing as they dab at the last bacon grease on their plates with wads of dried bread. You can come help me drag that whole mess on the east line. I got all those rocks to haul out. Bring your damned ponies up there tomorrow and do a little work for me for a change and not that damn Beidermann.

Heads down, without a word, they swallow the last of their food, and race away.

Without a word myself, I raise only a quieting hand to Harris, which to his quick temper is bad as a rebuke, and he rises from the bench, his eyes glancing elsewhere, face reddening to send the strawberry mark on his neck and cheek a dark purple; the mark being an inheritance from Ma's grandpa, an ignominious man of whom no one on her side speaks willingly, who carried that same mark. Of seven boys with that same blood, Harris is the only one with the mark. We watched him grow with it, a large and sturdy boy, sour as a pickle, with nothing of his brothers' humor and ease. Before he first tried shaving—and on the mark no hair grows—he already harbored in his breast a sinkhole of rancor. The question is there in my mind, and has been almost from the beginning; Does the mark bring the Devil, or does the Devil bring the mark?

Ma has her own explanation for her son's spleen: You must watch what you say to Harris, she says. He has a thin skin.

I know this, although I have never said it to Ma: if a man ties a red rag to a chicken's leg, every other bird in the flock will run in a minute to peck it to death. And I am sure in my mind that the marked chicken knows a moment before the murdering flock descends—it realizes in that moment that it is marked and sees what is coming. . . . That is the moment in which Harris lives.

I try telling myself: It is not enough to tolerate him, you must like him as well.

He pounds across the porch floor, slams the screen door.

JUNE 7. How deep is he now? The twins relay to me Beidermann's progress, or rather that of the vituperative Radke, and damned if I do not find some interest in their chronicle. Ten feet? Fifteen feet? Sandstone? Bedrock? Some of the twins' infatuation with the event is catching.

But they *will* go on. . . . This evening, as he washes up on the porch, Harris listens through the screen door and calls out: Why it sounds like Mister Beidermann himself is *making water*. Ho ho!

He comes in wiping his hands and slaps one of the unamused twins on the back; while the other boys, having little practice in enjoying Harris' cleverness, chuckle faintly.

Radke, it appears, now reaches one hundred fifty feet. And Beidermann has costs still ahead: the pipe itself, the pump, some sort of wind-driven mill to bring the water up—if it is there to bring up. Maybe Beidermann will indeed care to sell off a few fat heifers at a bargain price to his good neighbor.

JUNE 8. Across the room from my table Ma sorts rags for her next rug—or perhaps the one after that: quilts and rugs, they do not end. We are alone, the boys outside, on the porch perhaps, the twins quickly asleep, and I say: Well, Ma, maybe the lads will pick up some water-witching tricks from Beidermann. They could make some money on it, eh?

As lightly as I meant it, Ma does not take it so, as if she has thought this prospect through. Well, they are twins, she says in her calmest voice, busy with her rags; and so they have the special ways of twins. They know each other's thoughts. We have seen it since they were born. My cousin Bertha's twins had the same way, before they died. It marks twins, the different ways they have.

I look at her in surprise as she goes on: But money, no, if they have a gift, they cannot take money for it. No. A gift is pure and simple God-given, and he who receives it must give of it back.

Well, say I, taken up short by her strong opinions. It is a pity there is no money in it. But as for those marks—maybe I have one myself. How do I know? What is Gladys Krupp's mark—her goiter? Take old Beidermann; what is his?

Without a moment's thinking she says: No, you do not have one or anything near it. Yes, Gladys has her condition. And Leo Beidermann has the big finger of his right hand cut off. You know that. She glances at me in reproof and goes on, all the while tearing up one of my old shirts, tattered thin as paper, into strips one inch wide: No matter the gift, she says, if you take money for using it, it turns into a curse, a terrible curse.

I look over at her. This is not territory we have gotten into before. Well, well, I say. You sound so certain, you must have proof, eh, how this gift God generously hands out to people shy a finger from some fool accident, goes bad, eh? I want to hear about that awful curse.

Outside the kitchen on the summer porch I hear chairs drawn back to be tipped against the wall, to each side of the screen door, out of the light from the kitchen lamp. Otto and August have come to listen, having finished milking: a few mumbled words pass between them; then a little stirring—they are piqued that my sarcastic way may put Ma off from telling a fancy tale.

Calm as she pokes amongst her rags, Ma's mind is in full lope, and she says only: Don't be smart. Yes, I have proof. It was in my own family, which was my second cousin Ethel, who was a twin with Esther, who died of the whooping cough around three years. It was Illinois, and Ethel, just when she got her growth, found her gift. People knew it was there all along, her being a living twin, and it did come out, too, but it was not the water-witching, it was the healing—

That's fine with me, say I with a grand wave. It sounds like a better gift anyway—especially if you are only sick and not thirsty.

From the dark porch comes a snickering buzz which Ma ignores, perhaps does not hear, being intent on her rags and story. How Ethel came by it, she says, the poor girl was lost in the sloughs by where they lived for three days, gone picking berries, and everybody gave up hope for her. And then one of the old dogs, big old black one-eyed hairy thing that could kill a bear, which was out in the sloughs catching frogs or snakes, well, this old dog found her, and she came wading through those bogs holding the dog's tail, the both of them all stuck with burrs and—

You know something? I put in: I had an uncle once who used to say, Dog spelled backward is God, and he died a miserable death with screaming fits, yelling how sorry he was, which everyone figured meant he was sorry for saying that.

You might be sorry for saying that, too, says Ma mildly, as suppressed titters sound on the porch. She shoves the rags to the side of her rocking chair to make room for her feet, and says: Ethel was all bit by bugs and starved and sick from swamp fever and bloody from sawgrass cuts and swollen up with nettles, and she lay in a bad fever for seven days and six nights; and on the seventh night all her close kin gathered at her cot, as she appeared to be lost. And then—lo and behold—it was a miracle, and she was delivered, and woke up, and on her face was the smile of the purest angel—

Wait a minute, say I. Were you there?

Oh my, no, this happened before I was born. Cousin Ethel was an old woman when I knew her—fifty years maybe. But people were there who saw it all, my own ma saw it, and how Ethel had this smile like she had the queen's look at Heaven, and this smile never left her lips after that. She was made into a different person, like Gunnar Quist's wife, when she went crazy, became a different person. But Ethel was different in a good way. Nobody had ever seen anything like it. And then what happened was, a week after she rose up from her deathbed, well, that old dog who had fetched her from the sloughs, he stepped in a wolf-trap and snagged his leg about halfway up, looked to be broken. My ma saw it dangling. Ethel's pa, his name was Fritz, took up a single-tree to club the dog out of its misery, but Ethel threw herself on that dog and hung on and would not let her pa do that terrible deed. So Fritz figured to let her pet the dog a little and when she wasn't looking, he'd do away with it. But she fell asleep right on the porch, hugging the dog close and there was no way Fritz could knock it in the head without hitting his own daughter, too, so he just gave up. Now, in the morning, when Ethel and that dog woke up, why that old dog just walked away on every one of his four legs, pretty as you please. You could see where the fur was scraped, is all. His name was Hitch, and everyone said that now he could see out of his bad eye, too, which he never could before. He lived a couple more years—

A muffled chuckling comes from the dark porch, then a waitful silence.

Okay, say I, fulfilling the role my invisible audience expects of me: your cousin had the gift of life saving—of a dog. I would say that's a veterinary gift, but I want to know how it gets to be a curse.

She has finished my shirt, every usable bit of it in narrow strips by her slippers, and she starts on a flour-sack tea towel frazzled with holes. There is a lot to this story, she says. It is not so simple to tell in a minute. It is the whole life story of that woman, Ethel.

Ah then, let me not hurry the telling. Give us every glorious detail.

Quiet for a minute, Ma finally says: If you want to turn up your nose, that's fine, but then you should not ask me in the first place.

Again, the displeased stirring on the summer porch as Otto and August—and with a loud clump of boots someone else joins them, Henry perhaps—grow more impatient with my interruptions.

Ethel, says Ma, filled out into a good-looking woman. No one understood why she never got herself married, but she didn't. One thing, she had a mole on her chin, a big one, like the picture of the witch in the boys' fairy tale book. She went for a nurse in the army, traveled along the Arkansas border in the fighting, and there are stories of her saving a lot of lives there, too—

Wait, say I. Now you have made her into a double-marked woman—being a living twin, and now this mole. And, besides, being a nurse to soldiers does not mean a God-given gift for healing.

It was not just her being a nurse, it was more. When she come back from the battlefields she lived in White Bluff, which was her pa's place, and they had a neighbor, Hamm—they all moved to Minnesota right after— who had a boy, about the twins' age, his name was Alvin, and he come down with the typhoid. Well, she was a real nurse besides her gift, so Ethel went over to heat up some milk and honey and vinegar for him, and he was on his feet in one day. One day. Everybody else who caught the typhoid— one of the Hamm girls did—were laid up two months, even more. It was worse than the cholera. But in one day Alvin Hamm was up and walking.

I would not sell short the milk, honey, and vinegar, say I.

No, it was Ethel. Her touching him did it, her hand on his feverish brow—

Wait, wait, Ma, say I. The feverish brow—where are you getting this stuff?

Off the dark porch comes a deal of shuffling and coughs and muffled guffaws, the boys lurking there knowing as well as I that Ma, for all that she greedily reads her Bible and tiresome old Scott and those others—indeed, taught their reading to all our boys when the school board, with Krupp feebly running it, failed to find or afford a teacher—but still she has a softness for the ripe tales in the newspapers and magazines swapped with the Widow Jenssen every few months; and some measure of that latter reading, I would say, sneaks into her story.

My question ignored, she says: Now, having saved the Hamm boy, Ethel was called over to Minnow County, where there was a woman had a stillborn and the milk-fever come on her. This was a Polack woman, name of Anya something—I never could pronounce it. Well, now, Ethel was there for one day and one night, and that woman was on the edge of dying, but two days later she was on her feet and cooking for a whole threshing crew—twelve or fifteen men. And she herself vowed all the rest of her life that it was Cousin Ethel who did it—the cool touch of her hand on the brow. The Polack woman said it was like a smiling angel of mercy had come from a dream to rescue her. That's what she said, herself.

Ma, say I, admit to us: you have been doing some dreaming yourself, eh?

Ma looks straight at me. Yes, I have, she says; and none of them are dreams it would make you comfortable to hear about.

Silence from me, from the porch.

Now, says Ma, not long after Ethel raised that Polack woman up, she was called into the worst of the winter storms that part of the country had ever seen, to nurse a man, he was in the woods, cutting timber, who slipped and fell on his ax blade; the workers with him took him to a cabin where a woman and her little girls lived, which was closest to the woods. And one of the little girls—it was so brave of her—rode through that storm to fetch Ethel, and she come through this storm to the cabin and found this man with an awful cut across his stomach—terrible—so that his innards were pushing themselves out, like you get when you butcher a hog: a wonder that he had not bled to death already, but the men with him had tied him up with shirts and handkerchiefs. It was terrible, terrible, a test of Ethel's gifts like she had never seen. . . .

It is quiet now on the porch with the tale growing so grim; but calmly as before, Ma tears her rags, her voice thoughtful as she calls up these facts told to her, recollections of a distant time; blood and misery and horror of the past, remembered by the kin of victims, themselves remembered only for the pained and ugly awful moments of their lives. I have no sarcasm for this, and outside the dark door, Otto and August and whoever else has come up, wait with no more sound than the creak of their chairs.

Ma goes on, in the voice she would use to instruct the twins how to snap beans, and she braces back to slice her hand, rags dangling from it, across her lower belly. When Ethel saw this, she grew pale. Now, of course, she had tended terrible wounds in battle, wounds that ordinary mortals did not survive, which can be healed only by the mercy of God Himself. This man had a wound like that; out of it hung guts this long—Ma measures off a distance with a torn piece of an ancient curtain. All bleeding and smelling, the little girls crying . . . And Ethel lays her hand upon his feverish brow. . . .

Ma, say I, the story is growing too bloody by far.

She rips away, heedless of my voice, the summer porch in full silence now. No bugs hum in the corn, and in the scum beneath the cattle trough the toads hold their tongues; and we all wait for what this woman will say next: whatever mixture yet she will pull out of her scrambled dreams and memories and told-to tales of her kin's dark history.

There is more . . . Ethel lay her hand on the man's hot brow and smiled at him, that smile of hers. He was in an awful state. Yes, he was insensible, and could not see her smiling face, but yet he felt the coolness of her hand—

Ma, Ma, wait, Ma, say I. You are going pretty far here. . . .

—but he can see in his mind's eye, for God has given him this last gift of the dying moment, to see himself; he sees his soul oozing away through the terrible cut in his belly. The poor man—

Not for a moment has she ceased tearing her rags, with a heap of untorn cloth still at her side: every worn-out garment, every old sack or curtain, every swatch of canvas weathered enough to be pliable, every outused square of cloth passing through her hands ends here as raw material for rug or quilt: until doomsday she will be at her gathering and tearing—

She has not stopped her story: Ethel sees that this is a test of her, nothing less. All those days while the storm blows—a terrible storm, killing settlers and their wives caught out in it, and cattle from one side of the country to the other, all piled up and froze to death. And Ethel sits by the wounded man with her hand on his feverish brow all night, and the next day, too. And those brave little girls keep a fire going with nothing but cobs and hay, and the cabin gets so cold their own breath fills it up like a snowy mist, and in the morning, the fire gone down, they are so stiff with cold they can scarcely move. Now, the wounded man . . . he is warm under the buffalo robes and he is come back from death's door. He turns his face to Ethel, and he says: Who are you? And she says: My name is Ethel. And he says: No, your name is not Ethel, for you are an angel, and you have saved me. Now, reach your hand into the left pocket of my britches and take out what you find there. Do it! So she did as he commanded, to find that she held in her hand a five-dollar gold piece. The man on the cot says to her That is your payment for the miraculous healing you have performed upon me. And she says: No, I refuse it, I ask no payment. The gift I possess is payment for itself.

Here Ma breathes a long sigh of regret, and her voice changes back from Ethel's to her own. You see? It was too late. She had taken the money from his pocket and held it as her own in her hand. Too late. Her gift was corrupt the moment that money touched her hand. Do you see that, how it happened?

Ma is not looking at me, for she studies her rags; but I nod, saying nothing. I can say: No, I do not see, and let her explain. I can say: Yes, I do see. It makes no difference: there is nothing to see.

No sound from the porch; but in a minute a rumbling voice, which is clearly Harris'—so he is the one who has come during Ma's telling—and if he is speaking to his brothers his voice is not more than a long grumble which I cannot decipher.

But Ma is not finished: From that moment on, Ethel had no gift. It had flown out of her body, and she was an everyday person no more special than me. She could not heal a swatted fly. She had corrupted her gift and God took it from her, just like that.

She takes to sorting the torn rags now, dark colors in a pile on the left of her rocking chair, light on the right, each pile growing like a protective pillar. You may have heard my mother tell it, she says. She liked to teach a lesson from it, like she did with Bible stories. She knew Ethel and Esther, although she never knew our twins. But the lesson is there, still.

The lesson, say I. What lesson is that, then?

Why, that the twins cannot take payment for using their gift. It is God-given and cannot be bartered.

I hear Harris' simmering rumble, and he bellows: For Christ's sake, Ma! What are you talking about? Those boys didn't do anything. Beidermann did, with his damn wishbone. And God didn't lift a finger either. Maybe the Devil did.

Yes, says Ma, the Devil will surely put his nose in wherever he can, as I have explained.

It is clear to me, and it seems so to the boys, that we need explore this matter no further. All are quiet. Harris broods—even from the porch his doing so can be sensed; the other boys silently adrift in their own confusion; and myself at the edge of the bluff, like a preyed-upon animal pushed by its enemies, where it must jump into the unknown space below, empty space hidden in a fog.

At long last Ma rises from her chair to stand between her pillars of rags; and there is not a single thing, no twitch of a muscle, no roll of an eye, no curl of lip, to show that she differs from the woman she was this forenoon, this afternoon, this evening, or every forenoon, afternoon, or evening for however many years we wish to count back. . . . We have had a quarter-hour's story, imagined from her kinswoman's past; and that, having been spun out, leads her again to her kitchen, where, pushing aside her rags, she goes to rummage in the cupboard, to bring out a pie made yesterday from dried apples, and slicing it, she calls: Otto, August, Harris—without seeing if any of them is there to hear—If that cream is cooled off, you bring it in and have some with this pie.

Laying out this treat, she turns away for bed.

The boys hear, but no one moves to fetch the cooled cream; and in full appeal the pie rests upon the crinkled oilcloth, needing covering soon, as even in the lamplight the flies persist with a buzz that grows louder and louder.

JUNE 9. He has found his damned water, rather Radke the digger has—and who should receive the first handshake: he who guesses it is somewhere near, or he who draws it forth to see? The twins carry home their report so far after suppertime that Ma's scolding is vigorous enough to require that I add nothing, as they address their Johnny cake and beans. By the third mouthful they regain their enthusiasm, to proclaim the consummation of the Beidermann adventure. What they burn to report, none of their brothers but Harris stays to hear, all hastening to light a pipe at the corral or finally curry an unkempt horse. Harris holds his end of the table alone; at the other, the twins' forks send up a tinnish clatter to accompany their voices; and while Harris mixes and remixes his card deck, each card so much rubbed that the heraldic figures thereon are indistinguishable to all but their owner, who uses his privity to defraud his brothers in games in which the stakes are shares of Harris' chores; although no more, his deceit having been found out.

Come and see, then, beg the twins between mouthfuls.

I have seen water run before, say I.

But not water their hero Beidermann has wrested from the stubborn earth. This is water, Harris might say, which is the water of Beidermann's invention. . . . But the lads exhort and cajole, having been taught a little of the arts of persuasion and debate from books their own Ma read to them; and I assent. Tomorrow we will see what Beidermann hath wrought. As Otto says: You have the privilege, sir, of seeing the likes of Pharaoh's pyramids, and perhaps the Sphinx thrown in . . . and take a light team to bring back that hayrake which Beidermann borrowed and promised to return but never did.

JUNE 10. Yes, amidst the scattered rock and dirt left by Radke, there runs a little water upon a dry field where none ran before, where hay will grow now. At the twins' insistence I take a draught: it is water, warm, with iron in it. Beidermann has brought forth water; who would deny it? The twins race around the plank-buttressed shaft, a dance of water nymphs, Beidermann standing near and if he had a vest, his thumbs would be in the armholes and his chest thrust forth like a new father.

Congratulations to Mister Beidermann. I said it to him this noon; I write it here at midnight, a timely hour to mull over God-given gifts . . . or Devil's curses. . . . The toads are silent, the cicadas asleep, the animals at peace. From our bed Ma breathes loudly; for the years pass and it becomes less simple to draw each night's breath. So it is. . . . Beyond the dark I hear the poet:

Cuckoo, jug-jug, pu-we, to-witta-woo.

Beidermann's Place

OCT. 9. Cool and windy. Currying the black mare I see she is putting on her winter hair, as are all the cattle now. The boys bring in another wagonload of wood, this being the last left for cutting on the South Fork, so they report, but I will go out tomorrow to confirm this for myself.

Winter is coming, I tell Ma.

Yes, she says: as it always does.

OCT. 19. Mild and cloudy. The stock tank is iced over, and Otto takes an ax to it. A speckling of snow overlays all; and the banking of manure against the underpinnings of the house bears a skin of frost from inner moistness. The pump is freed with a boiling kettle, and Ma will soon be melting snow for her soft water.

. . .

OCT. 29. Cold and clear. Our bachelor neighbor Beidermann works the slim strands of cottonwood on the river five miles north; this as passable timber for his building, and the scrubby cedar in the draws thereabouts as firewood. For this endeavor he secures yet again the loan of my twins, who come in after dark to report that, far from doing the boys' work of trimming or leading the skidding team, they take on the man's job of handling Beidermann's crosscut saw; and while it is not an undertaking at which I would readily test them, still I know that they are capable, for they are already gaining some size, with promise to attain the muscular proportion of all my boys, this being a legacy of myself and their mother, who is a large-boned woman of some heft in her own right. They eat a man's supper and report that in the weeks ahead, when Beidermann returns to finish his cutting, they will go to help, if I permit, which I do; although wondering that the proud Beidermann, so full of self-sufficiency always, bothers himself to ask help for this task when he seldom does for greater ones. But Ma says the company of the twins pleases him, they being admirers of his easeful command of animals, and of his skills as hunter and trapper, and his forthright ways; and so, it now seems, of his woodsmanship as well. It would please me if they showed a similar heartiness toward the lessons in their books, or the chores on their own place.

NOV. I. Cold and sunny. A good snow the two days past, now stopping; and a full wheel of sun today, which casts a brilliance on the drifted prairie that pains the eye, yet gives an aspect of splendor, against which stand like spills of ink the loud crows and blackbirds brought to picking in our cattleyard by the cover laid over prairie range. Otto and I ride through the northern quarter toward Krupp's place, and find respectable forage there and beyond, the wind having scoured the bluffs of snow to allow the cattle access. Otto remarks on their fat and sturdy appearance, which promises they will survive if we do not suffer too severe a winter; for even the fattest of steers will go under if the Northers come too swift and many.

NOV. 17. Cold and cloudy. This day the twins again put their hand to Beidermann's cutting, and come in each with a jack-rabbit's hind foot, severed from an animal the mighty Beidermann felled with a throw of his ax: so the lads report defiantly, awaiting the scoffs of their brothers who grow weary of tales describing our doughty neighbor's varied talents. August suggests the twins would do well to contribute to our own cutting; but we have hands enough for that undertaking, with upwards of ten cords set by; so that even Ma, who is seldom ready to admit that sufficient firewood exists on Earth to forestall winter's chill, allows that the supply shows promise. But promise only, for there is never certainty in providing against the snowy onslaught with which the Almighty tests the strength of His subjects on this land; as He does through drouth and flood, fire and pestilence, hunger and plague, thus to weed out the weak, the improvident, and the unblessed; plucking from His land the proud and faithless—so many of those gone now, Gaustad, Baum, the Dutchman, and others who thrived only five years ago, and now the prairie moves to reclaim their old places. For all that our own root cellar is stocked with potatoes, beets, carrots, turnips and cabbages, the sheds filled with good hay, the granary and corncrib laden, the smokehouse hung with hams—for all that this gives the appearance of provision, yet it is only appearance. The Almighty eye bores deep: what It sees where we see plenty, no man knows.

DEC. I. Clear and windy. The venerable poet warns:

> *The piercing cold commands us shut the door,*
> *And rouse the cheerful hearth; for at the heels*
> *Of dark November comes with arrowy scourge*
> *The tyrannous December.*

Their clothes scabbed with snow, the twins reach home after nightfall, leaving Beidermann on his homeward journey at the point four miles west where it brings him nearest our place. They have the two geldings, trustworthy animals, got as colts from the sullen Dutchman, whose place south of Skiles went under from grasshoppers first, and then drouth and the madness of his wife; who told me when I claimed the colts to take what tools and lumber I desired, since there was no one else to pay money for them; and so I gave him another eight dollars, which he needed; although there was little for me to salvage other than a bit of lumber from his small cabin and a few boards from the roof of his sod barn, some torn harness, a cultivator useful for its parts, and a good logging bob-sled. The despairing Dutchman left only a grove of apple trees—a grove of *sticks* no higher than my elbow—which may have lived for half of one season. His intention was to return to Wisconsin and start afresh, God willing.

Tomorrow, the twins go out again with Beidermann, and they ask my permission to take a harness team so as to double Beidermann's haul, in that he wishes to complete his cutting before the snow deepens; and while I am the first of any to help a neighbor, it is not my habit to lend out my horses unless under my own eye or that of Otto or Henry; for I have seen good men, irreproachable in most aspects, perhaps out of ignorance and not willfully, misuse animals badly when it costs them nothing; so I promise I will come along with my team, which pleases them, that I will see them in their men's work at Beidermann's side.

DEC. 4 & 5 & 6. Snow, cold and stormy. This is the first night in three that the twins and I will sleep in our own beds, and the reason for it is a grim one—more than grim, indeed calamitous, for our neighbor Beidermann, whose grave misadventure calls for our prayers on his behalf, for all that the stolid Beidermann would never ask for them. How he fares we will not know until morning when, should the weather permit, we will go to see if the doctor has come through, and if Beidermann is with us still.

WE ARE ONLY NOW back from tending Beidermann's hungry stock, and it is late. All are sleeping now but for Ma, who sees me take down this book and says, Well, you are going to burn the midnight oil now, I suppose. It will wait until you have got some sleep. Do you think you will forget it? And with a poke at the fire, she goes to bed.

No, there is no likelihood of forgetting; but I have in me some of the same disbelieving wonder which the twins show over this disaster, and the particulars of it beg sorting through; for in it lies a lesson, surely, and the Lord would have us learn that lesson. Perhaps He even offered an augury that we in our human blindness failed to see; a premonition lost to us in that pale dawn of three days past when we set out to aid Beidermann as promised; our sledge running swiftly over the firm snow to the river site where he is cutting, as the twins cluck the team along at a goodly pace, within my cautions to mind the animals' capacities and not overuse them. There is no foreboding in this.

As we come up to the river, Beidermann is snaking trimmed logs through the snow-choked brush cluttering the outer bank, his splendid Percherons snorting white clouds, their teeth grinding on their bits, heads tossing to the clang of buckles and groan of leather, and their great hooves send the snow showering up with each step. Behind them, Beidermann holds the reins shoulder high, stepping quickly aside the skidding log, the legs of his trousers stiff with frozen snow; and the collar of his mackinaw, folded up about his stubbled chin, bears the white coating of his frozen breath. He unhooks the chain from the log, leaving it beside a scattering of others of similar size in the threshed-up snow.

Well, so I have a full crew today, he says, as if I am remiss in not coming on earlier days.

Yes, I say, I have my doubts those nags of yours can get this job done, so I have brought a team that knows how to pull.

He spits tobacco aside, and bares his teeth in a slender grin. Yes, he says, I have been thinking of scrapping them and getting a yoke of those cattle Krupp favors.

At this the twins laugh, at the absurdity of such a trade; for they have often heard Krupp's tales of the oxen kept by his father in Illinois; beasts that could outpull any team, as Krupp had it: Old Dick hauled that stoneboat easier than any three horses, or Old Dan pulled that cow out of the mud like he was on a Sunday stroll; although for all his nostalgia over oxen, Krupp himself turns out to be a mule man; he brags on his mules no less than his father's oxen, and when he had them at our threshing, it seemed to me he was beginning to look like them; which Ma said was an ugly thought, but did not disagree.

Where are them evil dogs of yours? I ask, not wanting to be surprised by their teeth in my leg.

By God, says Beidermann, but you are a tough customer to please. You do not like my team and you do not like my dogs. Is there anything else about me that you do not like?—But if he wants an answer he does not wait for it.—Well, I left them running a deer this morning at my place and if they caught up to it you will not see them around here.

He turns away to tie his handsome team to a sapling, and retrieves his ax from the sledge, and hefts it from hand to hand as its flared blade glints: he has shown it to me before—a tool from the Old Country, he claims, in a manner as to say it has magical quality.

Now I am going to trim up another few logs for your sledge, he says, and if you boys would not mind loading these here on that sledge of mine, why I would be much obliged. I am calling it quits here today. That timber up the line toward Jenssen's is too damned scrubby.

He plows off through the snow into the line of trees along the riverbank while the twins and I begin to hoist the snow-crusted logs onto the sledge. From behind the walls of brush torn awry by the passage of the horses and dragged logs, we hear the whack of Beidermann's ax.

THROUGHOUT THE FORENOON the clouds lower and the weather grows gray. We sit on the trimmed logs to take our dinner of the wurst and cheese and hardboiled eggs Ma has packed. Beidermann eats his meat and bread with lard without talking, and finishing, wipes his mouth with the back of his mitten and pronounces: It will snow some.

The twins receive this with the gravity they give all Beidermann's opinions, even ones as unremarkable as this, and stop kicking snow at one another to cast sober eyes to the sky and to Beidermann and to me—as if I might challenge Beidermann's certainty, as I am often more than willing to do, if only to deflect somewhat the twins' excessive admiration of him: and while I have not been much successful at this before, I lose more ground now; for Beidermann flatters them by requesting they take his team—his mighty Percherons!—to skid out the logs that remain. To be offered the reins of Pegasus would thrill the lads no more; as with dwarf hands on the leviathans' bridles into the woods they plunge, and with manly cries come thundering forth, a snubbed log pitching behind in a rain of scraped bark and ice, as the two leap nimbly through the whipping hazelnut branches and dead blackberry vines.

Beidermann's snow comes; with little wind the large flakes, fat with wetness, descend through the still sky in such abundant quantity as to obscure us from each other and muffle the sound of Beidermann's steady ax.

His sledge is near loaded; and I go to bring my team forward, to take on the last load, as the snow falls near as thick as fog, to mute the sound that now comes to my ears: a queer, grunting bellow, like the belly-deep groan of a man wrenching himself from a nightmare. (I have heard it since, in my mind, often.) I cannot see Beidermann; and the twins, at a distance into the brush, draw up at the ugly sound and look back to me, knowing I am not its source, but for assurance that no threat lies in it.

I cannot offer it; for I am no less alarmed than they, and it is with dread that I push through the brush to where the sound of Beidermann's ax has ceased.

He lies an arm's length from its bloodied blade; upon his side, on one elbow, like a man reclining at a Sunday picnic. But he lies on no pretty blanket upon shaded grass; but instead in a bed of trampled, dirty snow and torn branches, and he twists his face around through a screen of falling snow and in a quiet rage says, Now I have done it, for damned sure.

It is his leg, or foot, I think, for that is where a glancing blade would go with lightning certainty; as it did with my brother Emil in the Wisconsin woods, myself a terrified lad no older than the twins now; with Emil leaning on me, dragging his half-foot, the fat part of that leg tied off tightly with the thong from the useless boot, to leave the snow spotted with blood for three miles until we met the old man coming with a team for the fence rails we were cutting.

But with Beidermann it is not his foot, for he will maintain singularity even in so dire an event. He holds his left hand, from which half of one finger is long since gone from some happening he has never remarked upon, like a shield over his red lower belly near his loins; and I see now the soaked mackinaw beneath that hand where the flakes of snow melt on touching. He has slipped, then, with his swing, the wet snow at his feet giving no purchase, or the incomplete hand giving an incomplete hold, and fallen on the razor edge of his Old Country ax blade as it glanced off the gnarled joint where branch meets trunk. . . . Fallen on his ax! For the doughty Beidermann, so humble a misadventure!

The stubby whiskers of his chin catch the falling flakes, and his eyes watch mine; not fearfully, I think, but to gauge by my look the full measure of his misfortune: but no, he means to catch panic or unsureness in me, as if I might flinch away like a girl, unmanned by the sight of the stain which spreads from his coat to the mounded snow, where it turns from red to pink.

At my shoulder as I kneel to see, the team restless behind them, the twins freeze in an awful silence, stunned at Beidermann's fall; this giant figure to them, a certain kind of man unlike others they know, with his grand tales of buffalo, and digging gold in the Western hills, and his lessons to them in bringing a wild horse to hand, or in finding water in desert sand. More easily can they imagine their father fallen, or one of their grown brothers.

With his stub finger, Beidermann struggles to undo the buttons of his thick coat, and when I reach to help, he continues as if I am not there, and pulls back the skirt of his mackinaw and his wool outer pants, where the pants beneath reveal a bloody slash in the fabric just below the waist and a little to the right side. He unbuttons the suspender there to push the pants down, and the blood comes freely over his hand as he raises himself on his elbow, the better to see.

I have done it, he says, God damn it all.

I bend close, and it is a wicked sight: not a clean cut but more a gouged tear, as a consequence of a twist of the flared blade as he plunged his weight onto it. Nested in that tear a shiny purple bulge pulses; from the outer edges of its eruption blood wells in easy surges. On this glistening mound the falling flakes melt, and the odor is that of a butchered steer, or hog, or chicken—all alike in the end, none so different among living creatures as to claim singularity—and I am filled with wonder that this odorous patch of Beidermann's insides hopes to push itself free as if it has awaited this moment for as long as Beidermann has been a man. It is disquieting to my own heart, and to the twins, bending to see, it can be no less; for all that they have seen guts before, but always those of creatures whose mortality is certain.

This has a serious look to it, I say; and it is as if my saying so makes Beidermann need to prove me wrong: holding coat and trousers free of the wound, he rises briskly to one knee—for all the world as if he will take to his feet and stride off as if he suffers nothing worth more attention than that already given it. Above the soughing snow, I hear the twins sigh in awe: *now* he proves their estimate of him.

But he is still human. His motion excites the blood at the edges of the blockage, and before he can stand and empty himself through the hole the ax has made, I lay my hand on his shoulder to bear him down. He looks sharply at me, irked, but that look passes: his face is gray and sagging, but more, I think, with wrath than suffering.

Get me something to tie this up, he orders.

I will do you better than that, I say; and tell the twins to roll the top logs off Beidermann's sledge, so that five or six lay even, on which a man can rest; and as they do so, I take some flour sacking I have for a handkerchief and offer it to Beidermann to cover his wound. He rises, as the twins watch in disbelief, and takes a step toward the sledge; but now his pain seizes him and cants him onto me like a man with one leg. He holds the rag against his side, and the seepage from it stains portions of my own clothing as I lean him against the snowy logs that make a bed on the sledge. The twins come close to help, but there is no way to do so.

Hitch up his team, I tell them, and tie our team to that back post.

They jump to do that; as with lessening help from Beidermann himself, who is swearing, I drag him fully onto the logs, and my-self take a crossways seat behind him, that he can recline his head against me.

Go to my place, he says.

No. Jenssen's place is closer, I tell him. The Widow can fix you up until we can get the doctor.

At the front end of the logs sit the twins, with their feet dangling at the horses' hooves: one holds the reins like glass, the other holding down our saws and axes, Beidermann's bloody ax amongst them. The first clucks in a dry voice to the team, steering it free of the trees and down the sloping bank, across the ice, then to heave up the sharp western bank, as the track leads onto the prairie over the tops of sage and tall weeds poking through the drifts, the horses' snowy haunches rolling from the ponderous

trot they take up when the shallowness of the snow allows. I grip
Beidermann's shoulders to prevent jarring of his head: his face
grows near as white as the snow falling upon it.

We will make it by dark, I tell him.

Ahhhh, he sighs. By God, I have done a few foolish things in
my life, but this one takes the cake.

I have seen worse things happen to good men, I say, thinking
of my own brother and the blood poisoning that took his life; and
decent Swede Jenssen, toward whose place we hasten, gone under
in two days from injuries on our binder; and I tell Beidermann,
You will be as good as new when we get you into a bed and fetch
Doc Entwhistle to take a look at you.

He grunts, or groans. Yes, he says, and to get him out here in
this weather I will have to sign over my place to him.

Well, I say, he is not a bad man, when he is sober.

He says nothing for half a mile, then whispers hoarsely: Your
boys handle that team nicely.

That they do, I say.

They have the team moving swiftly over high ground, avoiding
the undulate drifts where they can, and where they cannot with
slapping reins send the horses breasting through to clearer ground.
For all the snow, there is less wind than we have a right to expect,
as if the Almighty has sufficiently afflicted our wood-gathering enterprise, and withholds a full-grown storm. Beidermann's calamity
is the limit of His test of us for this time; for it is not simply a foolish mistake, as Beidermann would have it, but surely a test; a trial
given Beidermann as a consequence of prideful behavior and the
arrogance bespoken not only in his words, but in his manner of

doing, and attempting overmuch—this man who bites off plenty every time, no matter that he shows ability to chew with the best: for there are circumstances the Lord cannot overlook, and He is absolutely bound to answer Earthly arrogance with its Divine twin—His own mighty power; so that of His might there may never be left a doubt in the minds of bystanders who, observing unpunished bullheadedness, will be tempted to overreach likewise.

This, I know too well, as the signs to me have been many and various; from so small an admonition as the failure of a spring to flow, to the dire blow of not many winters past, when He took our only daughter: the child gone so young she lacked a name, although Ma and I have given her a secret one; and thereby decimated our clan; for this little child, if only for a tick of time, made us ten in number: the only daughter, gone as a tiny infant, claimed because I had pushed beyond the limit of the Lord's tolerance in my ambition—no, more than ambition—lust, it was, for greater possession, for laying hands on more, and accumulating land under my name and my boys' names, as far as a man could ride in a week's time. I wanted no boundaries: for it is boundless, a man's hope, and cannot easily be checked, and yet it always is, for the Lord will in time balk. And so she was taken from us, in the common way—losing breath in the night, her little body cold at Ma's side in the morning. . . .

Far above in dreamless sleep
Safe in Christ's tender fold,
My baby doth serenely rest,
From winter's chill and cold. . . .

The snow hastens dusk, and it grows colder; but now a shadow looms. We have come upon the hill of snow that is Jenssen's sod barn, the house a stone's throw beyond.

ABOUT ANNA JENSSEN I have never shied from admitting my doubts, for all that she has done a job in running Swede's place after he went under, and bringing up their two young girls: still she is such a scrawny rail of a female, full of silly giggles and shrill complaint, being just the style of woman suited to keep those flocks of noisy geese. But now, having delivered the wounded Beidermann to her door, and watched her way with him, I wonder if my opinion is not too limited; for she reveals a competence and easy manner concealed before by scattered behavior; and whether this derives from a knowledge of the nursing trade discovered as a girl on the Missouri border, or if it is summoned from her out of a particular female concern for the vulnerable Beidermann, I cannot say. For certain there are enough rumors and gossip about the two of them; one report running so wild as to have her carrying his child: this unfounded, for as Ma said, time would tell; and it did not: although Ma herself vows there is a fancy between them, which, with the touch of the busybody in her, she would like to help advance. But if something goes between the two I have not observed it, nor do I ask to; for all that I am willing to believe that a woman in the Widow's severe circumstances would readily fancy a bachelor as agreeably fixed as Beidermann.

In the moment the Widow opens the door, wearing Swede's sheepskin coat, her long narrow nose tipped red with a cold, she knows what we have brought. She sees the slumping Beidermann on the logs white with snow, and I fear she will screech; but she does not, and at once appears to gather in the true degree of the affair; and her long mare's face, too often alight with a misfitted twinkle when men are at hand, is sober and keen, as if calamity clears her head like the camphor I smell in the room behind her, where her two girls, with running noses, stand fearfully.

Was it the horses? she says: for it was Swede's team that pulled our binder over him.

No, I say, it was the ax.

Without pause for more talk, she hooks one of Beidermann's arms around her shoulders while I take the other: he protests, half pushing me away, and whispering and muttering, but what he says I cannot hear; perhaps it is for the Widow, a private message, as she steers him to the girls' bed; and with quiet urgency and no feminine shyness sets to stripping the bloody clothes away, leaving a strip of the inner pants to cover his loins; and over one shoulder directs the youngest girl to fetch clean rags and the pot from the stove; while I tell the twins to put up Beidermann's and our team; and over her other shoulder the Widow instructs the older girl in how to move the stock in the barn to accommodate all.

Beidermann lays like a bull in this room, breathing deeply but unspeaking beneath the Widow's hands, his presence filling more than the bed. It is not a small house for this region, two rooms joined by a doorless arch, all from pine Swede's brother freighted in from Minnesota; the walls all papered; all but the far corners visible to me as I sit at the table with a lamp under which Swede and I played more than one game of cards.

The Widow offers womanly sounds of comfort as she sets to bathe Beidermann's wound in a solution of mercury, and overlays it with a pad of cotton soaked with carbolic acid and olive oil; all done with an easy, practiced hand.

It needs sewing up, she says.

That will have to wait for the doctor, then, I say.

Beidermann tries to raise his head to look. If I have seen him without a hat before, I do not remember it: his hair falls away from his head evenly on all sides, thick and black as an Indian's.

No, it will not wait, says the Widow.

From her sewing box she brings forth her large needle and cotton thread, quickly bathes both in chemicals from her jars, and with one hand taking its widest reach with fingers and thumb, brings together the torn edges of the wound and begins her stitchery. Beidermann stonily eyes the ceiling beams, his mouth so clamped that the stubbled cheeks pucker. The Widow takes a slow pull on the thread, steadier of hand than I would expect. The twins and the two girls come in, and stop shaking snow off themselves to watch without a sound.

I have seen that done once before, I say into the lamp-lit silence: and I tell them of when as a youth I watched a ferryman, a black Norwegian, sew up a knife slice on his own knee with a fishing line as he vowed the while that horse hair would be better. While I do not say so, his workmanship was no more crude than the Widow's, although it takes a hard man indeed to ask that such make-shift surgery look as clean and pretty as a cross-stitched sampler. Looking over the Widow's shoulder in the dim light I tell her it is a masterful piece of work, and to Beidermann I pass a jest, that he is darned up more neatly than the toe of my sock; but he does not respond nor look at me.

You will have to bring the doctor soon, the Widow says to me, and in a lower voice: I have my doubts about blood poisoning already.

She casts a troubled look at Beidermann, who pants irregularly like a downed ox, his face reddening, perhaps as signal to the on-set of fever.

We will fetch him from Skiles in the morning, I say. One of the boys will go—Henry or Otto.

We will go, Pa, clamor the twins as one; but I raise my hand against it; for all that they are lads of fortitude, it is a half day's ride, and I choose not to experiment whether two children can persuade the crotchety Entwhistle, in his cups more often than not, to attempt the ride back through wicked weather: whereas Otto, should the physician offer an excuse, is by himself capable of extorting a supply of morphine or other helpful medicine, or even rising to the temper with which he was born and fetching the old croaker along by the seat of his pants.

Beidermann is talking, as if in sleep: I was fixing to butcher that hog . . . he mutters.

What? I ask. Well, we will do that, all right, when you are on your feet again, eh, boys?

The twins affirm that we will, and Beidermann has no more to say. The Widow moves the lamp, to leave him in darkness, and he seems to sleep; as she cooks us an agreeable supper of ham and turnips, with a batch of molasses candy to divert the children. All this disposed of in good order, we ready our beds: the twins and I under cowhides on the floor, and the two girls head-to-toe with the Widow in her bed, before which she hangs a flannel blanket for privacy. In the night I twice hear her coming out in the cold to look to Beidermann's comfort.

LONG BEFORE FIRST LIGHT, the Widow is up, and while I fix the fire, she washes Beidermann's wound, as the girls cook bacon and beans. When we have eaten, while the twins harness the teams, I go to Beidermann's side. I cannot say that he is sensible of me: his eyes roll upward and away, and with dried lips he murmurs so that I can scarcely hear—*the beast thou saw*. Or so I take it: it is something biblical, and nothing I have heard before from Beidermann: in his calamity he transcends himself; or it is the hog that goes unbutchered invading his feverish dream.

You hang on, I tell him, and we will do all the rest.

Well, go and do it, then, says the Widow, retrieving the waspish aspect of her disposition displayed so often as poor Swede's wife, but kept concealed as the tender nurse to Beidermann, which she has been the night past.

WITH STRENUOUS NORTH WINDS behind and a heavy sky above, we retrace our blown-over trail of yesterday, and are soon at the river, and in two hours more at our place, where we relate at length the tale of Beidermann's misfortune; this told less by me than by the twins, in bursts of breathless wonder, that this could happen to their Beidermann.

It is a terrible thing, says Ma, but you were right to take him to Anna's. She has a good sense in those things. I remember. . . .

But here she falls silent, and if what she remembers is the Widow's nursing of Swede as he went under, or her midwifely ministrations at the birth of our doomed little daughter, that is left unsaid.

Otto takes my sheepskin coat for the ride to town, and although it is my contention he will do as well on snowshoes, given the fall of new snow and promise of more, yet he takes the black mare, vowing to keep to the bluffs on Krupp's boundary, which the wind sweeps clear.

The twins ask to accompany him, Otto being not unwilling for the companionship; but the two of them and Harris as well must aid me in returning Beidermann's team to his place and in feeding his stock, which has gone untended too long now. Harris follows with a fresh team for our return, as I set Beidermann's mighty Percherons to pull the sledge bearing the logs which, under a mantle of snow, carry the stain of their master's frozen blood.

The twins are called to service soon enough: for Beidermann's treacherous wolf-dogs, savage even with full bellies but now long unfed, come bounding through the wind-swirled snow like the very hounds of Hell, confounded only momentarily by the sight of their master's team under a strange hand. They head for Harris with blood in their eyes, until the twins jump amongst them happily, I would say; for they admire these beasts no less than does Beidermann—hollering words of some peculiar low Dutch which they have heard Beidermann use to curtail them. The dogs reluctantly haul up in slobbering puzzlement, yet lurk menacingly near, as if to ambuscade whoever moves incautiously; the boldest of the pair a three-footed brindle bitch, one paw lost to a trap, which injury has taught her not a jot of respect for the human race, as she is the most slaveringly vicious of this foul pair.

Boys, Harris calls to the twins. You keep them egg-suckers well clear of these horses, or I will put a load of buckshot in their hinders without a second thought!

Knowing Beidermann's ways with the snarling brutes, the twins go after the frozen offal and bones hanging high in a log lean-to by the house, the brutes yelping and slithering in the snow, as the twins engage them in murderous teasing play, the animals baring teeth and promising to spring for a throat, but never doing so. It is a wonder these killers have not assaulted the hogs or calves and already made their own meal.

Harris and I give them a wide berth as we unhitch Beidermann's horses, which plow a path through the snow to their barn, where I follow down the long alley, past the pens of bawling calves and cow stalls. It is a structure of enviable size, Beidermann's barn, in the construction of which the twins have, of course, lent their hand, as they have in the digging of his well, and the raising of his windmill.

Harris, having fed the horses, aids me with Beidermann's three milkers; and, setting aside part of the milk for the hogs, we carry the remainder to the calves skirmishing in their pen, bawling with hunger: butting and slobbering they skid to their knees on the manure-slippery floor, and plunge their heads into the pails, slopping milk to the floor, where it steams in the cold.

As the frantic bleating of the calves diminishes, I hear the growing howl of the wind; and when Harris comes back from the hog pen, the twins following from the chicken house, he says, It is kicking up out there, in case nobody has noticed.

Beyond the barn door the wind sucks up old snow off the drifts and sends it to mix with the needle-points of new snow descending aslant from a sky now dark. Beidermann's house is only a shadow, seen when a seam occurs in the driven sheets of snow.

Well, boys, we will not chance this, I say. Put our team in the barn with enough hay for the night, and make certain those dogs cannot get at them. We are not going anywhere soon, if I read this right. Let us hope Otto gets through.

For all their distaste of biting wind, the horses balk at entering a strange barn—a little of which bashfulness I find in myself when we hasten through the storm to Beidermann's door, through which I have never passed; for the only times I have visited Beidermann's place, our business has been outside, and Beidermann found no occasion to invite me within.

My own reluctance, however, does not restrain the twins, who have acquired ease around Beidermann's place and are first inside, eager to build a fire, for it is solid dead cold within: they know where under the snow the wood is piled—they have helped to pile it there—and dash to fetch it.

Ahead of me, Harris, stamping the snow from his boots, looks once around and says, He has fixed himself a nice place, then.

He has indeed! I am caught by surprise and, soon, a little envy; for while I expected a rough bachelor's accommodations, in the style favored by other crude and unsubtle loners, wretched hutches, barely enough to prove up their land; not so with Beidermann. Not so, by any means; for he has furnished his two rooms in an exceptional manner, from hooked rugs made of old overcoat strips to chintz curtains hanging at the two windows—a woman's touch, perhaps; but what woman? I look around, compelled by what I know of Beidermann to make an inventory; for everything within these whitewashed walls is a surprise, like finding a spring of sweet water in the desert, which might be commonplace elsewhere, but here astonishing.

A nutmeg grater hangs from one of a row of nails above the square iron stove in which the twins have their fire sprouting, and next to it a blue enameled spoon, a potato masher, an iron ladle; and beneath these a pine-board shelf supports stone jars of varied size, labeled in fancy script: *Sugar, Salt, Soda.* In the coldest corner by the door, above a speckled pail with its dipper held in half a foot of solid ice, hangs a saddle of venison, doubtless from the same animal of which the twins brought home a portion a month earlier. On the wall above the table, at which Harris takes a seat, is a cross-stitched hanging which bears the legend *Endureth All.* Who has sewn it? In the far room, Beidermann's bedroom, his suspenders hang from a wooden peg above his bed. His bedstead is brass! And it is a featherbed, covered by a flannel blanket and cowhide. From two more pegs are neatly hung a spare shirt and trousers; and to their side a shelf holds a dozen books, one of them a Bible, one of Leatherstocking's tales, another of myths, and two volumes in German. On a little table rests an uncased fiddle—it is finer than the warped one I own—and on the wall above it, next the grandfather clock that is stopped from lack of winding, hangs a picture of birds perched in a flowering tree. I am put in mind of a certain foreign bird species, the male of which constructs an intricate and ornate bower, and struts preening before it until a female, attracted by his artistry, succumbs.

Harris offers advice to the fire-builders, but they already have a blaze under way. Outside, the wind roars, falls to a murmur, roars again, to push a sifting of snow beneath the window frames and stuff the smoke down the chimney to puff from the seams of the stove. Beidermann's little castle trembles before the blast: his suspenders sway on the peg. I am not easy here, trespassing on Beidermann's secret empire; but we are trapped in it by the storm: not even the rugged Beidermann would ask a man to face the prairie in a Norther.

If Beidermann goes under, who will get this place? asks Harris. Who indeed? I have no answer.

While the twins make biscuits and Harris cooks up beans and bacon, I light Beidermann's etched-glass lamp against the cold shadows. In the wall cupboard Harris finds a jug of whiskey tucked behind a dozen pieces of glazed china—plates and cups, all bearing a pattern of perching birds and appearing long unused, perhaps never used: but we take our supper off tin plates at my order, for all that Harris fancies the china; as, indeed, he fancies the whiskey; of which, despite his importuning, I deny him more than a single drink, which he makes such a greedy one that I grab the jug away, much to his irritation. He is growing into a crude man, Harris: as the youngest son but for the twins, he believes little deference or privilege comes his way; and when he does not carp, he glowers: not a day—indeed, hardly an hour—goes by that does not hold disappointment for him, which he quickly voices.

Beidermann's elegant bedstead being inadequate for the four of us, I give it up to Harris and the twins; and in Beidermann's handsome buffalo robe roll up beside the stove, to listen for a long time to the wind slapping the house and howling in the distance: its ferocity I think excessive, for if man needs reminding of his insignificance on Earth, a storm one-tenth of this would suffice. . . .

At first light, for all that a brisk wind sweeps steadily from the north the strength has gone out of it, and no snow falls, so that the morning lies brilliant, in perfect cold: the drift against Beidermann's door reaching to our heads, it seems easier to tunnel than shovel clear, but at last we thresh our way to the barn to feed Beidermann's livestock and retrieve our team. We would hie ourselves home, but it is slow going for the horses, who plow a deep valley through the snow, until we strike the bluff by the river and the icy ground offers faster travel. Here we come across a frozen heifer of Beidermann's which has been chewed upon, and even more such may be buried half-chewed in the snow-filled gully. Harris says it is coyotes, although I think it is not beyond Beidermann's fiendish dogs themselves to do the trick. Tomorrow, on his way to tend Beidermann's stock, which will be his daily duty for a time, Harris vows to lace the carcass with strychnine, so that we might discourage such scavenging.

The day is mostly gone when, to Ma's great relief, we arrive; although we are still worried if Otto has outwitted the storm. When the boys are all in bed, I tell Ma of Beidermann's singular bachelor residence, describing it from curtains to china, for I know she will take a womanly interest in the refinement and elegance of it. But if I expected her to be surprised, she is not; and says only, The poor man.

DEC. 7. Cold and clear, windy. Early we are shoveling paths to all the pens, the wind driving snow back in all the while; and after chores, having given in no less to my own concern for Beidermann's welfare than their entreaties, the twins and I set out for the

Widow's place, bearing a pot of Ma's special stew for the invalid. An hour along, we come upon a welcome sight in this vast expanse of snow: it is Otto on the black mare, coming briskly toward us.

He is crabby with the cold, his cheeks a little frozen; but he has done his errand, and reports delivering the doctor in good order, with not much complication; having waited in Skiles at Rasmussen's stables for the storm to abate, that occurring in fine coincidence at the very time Doctor Entwhistle sobered sufficiently to ride.

We are eager for his report on Beidermann, and it is more sanguine than I expected; for all that Otto reports that Entwhistle, before hastening back to his jug the moment the weather cleared and he had extracted twelve dollars for his service, offered neither a strong yea or nay as to Beidermann's immediate prospects; although Otto has no doubts.

That Beidermann is an ugly ox, he says. He looks to me unkillable. He wanted me to drive him home. You will see for yourself.

He is off for the warmth of our house, pleased for the decent trail our team and sleigh have broken; in turn, we follow his path to the Widow's, where, approaching her door through banks of snow shoveled out as high as the horses' heads, I wonder, from Otto's description of the invalid's hardiness, whether Beidermann himself has not risen to do the shoveling.

He is in bed where we have left him; but presents a changed and surprising appearance: his hair is cut, neatly shorn all around at the ear to show the white and pink of his head, like a sheared sheep.

Hullo there, boys, he says, sounding nowhere near death, nor looking it. His face is somewhat drawn, and his position stiff on the mattress: he is a little bashful, but whether from his helplessness or his haircut, I cannot tell. The house is exceedingly warm, as if the Widow would burn her whole winter's wood for Beidermann. She clucks and fusses to straighten the covers he pulls aside in turning to see us.

You come to fetch me home then, eh? he says with hope; although clearly his readiness to leave signals neither a miracle from Entwhistle nor an exceptional spontaneous reclaiming of health, but more a desire to flee the Widow's fussy caretaking; which she continues hard at, bustling about, ordering her girls to boil some coffee for me as she lurks over Beidermann like one of those brooding hens with which she hatches out her goose eggs. For all his protests that he wants none, she fills his cup with Ma's stew, and smooths back what wild black hair she has left him; his demurrer to this being feeble, with little of the full Beidermann orneriness, as if he knows she must show her handiwork, like a woman who will display her new quilt to a friend.

It was money wasted to have Entwhistle, Beidermann claims; for in his opinion, as he says, Anna can do anything he can.

Does the Widow blush? I think so, as she busies herself to bare Beidermann's middle and bathe it with the black tar-smelling liquid Entwhistle left as proof against blood poisoning: she dabs it tenderly over a swollen tumor of shining scabs, which the twins push forward to wonder at.

He will have a lump there, says the Widow in a teacherly way. Like a rupture. But see, it is healing over already. The doctor says none of his innards is cut. It is God's miracle.

That may be. Her own husband went under from cuts and bruises of less severe appearance than this injury of Beidermann's;

but it was loss of blood that did Swede in. We could not stop it—that being not merely our selfish apology but Doctor Entwhistle's opinion as well: we could not have stopped it; and so suddenly did Swede go, being on his last legs when we got him home, that the Widow had no opportunity to practice her nursing skills upon him. For all that Beidermann appeared no better than Swede when we hauled him in three days earlier, now, as if he is chosen in a way denied Swede, he bids fair to recover.

The Widow plumps up her goose-down pillows under Beidermann's shoulders, as he again declares his readiness to travel—he would go right now, in my sleigh. He makes a demand of it: no polite request from Beidermann.

Shoot, I say, and lean over to give him a wink, if I was in your shoes, I would not be so eager to leave the bed and tender care of a good-looking woman.

The Widow raises her whinnying laugh. Beidermann's face darkens: his helplessness baffles him. He says, No, I mean to go.

Well, then, I say, if that is what you mean to do, let me give you my straight opinion, which is that at this stage of the game your best bet is not to get out of that bed. There is no call to court disaster. And if you are worried about your stock, well, there is no cause for it. My boys are doing your chores, and you will have to admit that they are considerable fellows, and do a bang-up job at what they tackle, which is the way I have raised them. By God, they even have those vicious hounds of yours eating out of their hands.

The patient gives me a sullen look. I do not like to put a strain on you, he says. You have chores of your own.

I have a whole houseful of boys to do them, I say; but I feel I am boasting again, for he has nothing like them in his house. With this weather they have time on their hands.

Beidermann stares in silence at the ceiling beams, his whiskery jaw clamped, and at last says, If I can get over to my place, I can do all right by myself.

Well, that is surely true, I say, and I note that the arrogance is gone from his voice: he speaks wonderingly, like a man asking a question about matters he has not thought of before, and of which he knows nothing.

I always have, before, he says.

I wonder if he has at last come upon a different notion of himself. Not only is it the Widow's hair-shears and beguiling pats he wishes to escape: God has visited the proud Beidermann, and he is beholden—and not to me, as he thinks. His leathern face draws down mournfully as if he relinquishes the vision of himself in his particular life, seeing now that it is furnished no more by china and lacy curtains than by reckless vanity. With his new-cut hair bristling against the Widow's pillow, he looks upon the fact that he is not the only man on Earth who can throw corn to hogs.

Beidermann looks on bleakly as the twins and I depart. From the door I call to him, A few more days and we will fetch you back to your place in fine style.

I suspect that when we do, I tell the twins, the Widow will have dug out Swede's old razor, and have Beidermann shaved just as pretty as you please.

HE WAS HEADED WEST at an angle to the constant wind, and not until a whirling dust-devil slapped back his hat brim did he catch the first scary sniff. The black mare—straightaway alert—caught it when he did: her nostrils flared, and she pulled her trick of taking the bit, lying back on her haunches and wheeling left. Beidermann wiped the grit from his eyes with one hand, and with the other kept hold just enough to let her swerve to catch the foreboding scent full on. She hesitated, trembling, judging it.

To the north now, on the mid-forenoon horizon, Beidermann saw thin gray skeins like wisps of river fog in autumn. They lay off toward Schneider's place—unlucky Schneider. The plain that inclined for miles in that direction dipped enough to hide signs of Schneider's buildings—if that was where the smoke came from.

He was as edgy as the mare now, uncertain whether to go on to old Praeger's place to fetch the boys for help on his irrigation flue, or turn aside and ride down to where the river bowed west, to see what was down there.

It seemed to him unlikely that the fire had hit Schneider's place or even come close: there would have been some alarm—shots fired, riders afield. But it was quiet on all sides, except for the whistle of the wind and the mare's blowing.

Now the few gray wisps he had glimpsed tattered in the wind, and he watched to see if they would reappear. The odor of smoke faded, too, and the mare calmed down. Beidermann waited, looking down the long slope. . . .

IF IT WAS what it looked like, Schneider could file another notch in his bad luck streak. Two years in a row. Last fall, no more than two miles south, Beidermann had helped one of Schneider's boys drag a fresh-split steer across a tenacious seam of fire that moved through the blue-stem grass nearly as fast as the horses—with a rope from each saddle-horn tied to a rear leg of the cadaver—could haul the bleeding baggage. He'd grabbed one of Krupp's ponies, having left his team tied far downwind to hasten afoot when he spied Krupp and Schneider and his two boys slapping gunnysacks to no effect on the furious blaze. When the worst of it was knocked down and he had cut his rope from what was left of the steer rather than knock through the crusted blood to find the knot, he turned the horse back to Krupp. The stunned beast hobbled away with charred and stinking hooves: a near cripple ever since, grumbled Krupp, who, even though the flames weren't near his place that time, came away a two-way loser: a crippled horse; and it was his steer that young Clarence Schneider had shot, it being the nearest and fattest. It took a while before old

Schneider, distracted as he was by the loss of his last hay cutting, remembered to make up Krupp's loss, Krupp carping all the while, of course.

Although he told no one, Beidermann suffered a loss of his own in that fire: his wool britches grew so overheated that the threads in the seams turned to fluff, and at home that night when he stretched to get off his horse, damned if his pants didn't fall half to pieces. . . .

He had come up on that fire while on his way to the Widow Jenssen's place—just as this time he was headed for Praeger's: best he stay home in fire season—and by the time they'd knocked it down, the forenoon was completely shot for plowing the Widow's new firebreak, as he had promised to do. Years before, her late husband, Swede, had put one in, but the Widow worried that it was too narrow and too close to the house anyway, what with the fires getting more and bigger every year. Beidermann offered to expand it, an easy job for his big team; for although the Widow and her girls, with the help of one drunken hired man or another, did most of the work on her place, sod-breaking was one thing she traded for.

Although it was too late for Beidermann to do the job that day, he came to do it two days later, bringing with him a few yards of brown cloth he had traded for in the spring with a peddler out of Minot who needed shoes on the shambling gelding that pulled his high-sided wagon, which reminded Beidermann of his mother's old kitchen cupboard, but on wheels. . . . From that stiff material the Widow had sewn him a pair of pants nicer than the ones he'd burned off in Schneider's fire. . . .

. . .

THE SMOKE HAD DISAPPEARED. Beidermann saw only the cloud-
less sky. He pulled the black mare around, onto the path toward
old Praeger's place, and set off, the suspect piece of landscape
over his left shoulder: he kept glancing back, but there was nothing but miles of downward slope.

There could be good reason there was nothing to see now, he
thought: in the first place, it might not have been a fire he'd
seen. . . . Or even if it was, it had burned itself out, having started
in some area without grass enough to sustain it. . . . Or perhaps
Schneider or someone had already knocked it down. . . . Or it was
Schneider's boys firing up an old straw stack or heap of this-
tles. . . . Or it might be some old line cabin or wood fence set afire
by renegade Indians—there was always talk of that possibility, although he hadn't seen any of it.

For a half-mile or more, casting a look back from time to time,
he went along toward Praeger's. He knew how fickle those bastard
fires could be. In one, the smoke might carry from one horizon to
another, warning everyone for miles to wet down the chicken-
house roof and bury the family Bible in the root cellar. In another,
it might sneakily hide itself, and a man might look up from hoeing
his potatoes and a dozen rods away discover his whole wheat field
afire, so close he could feel the heat against his head.

Or a man's animals by queer behavior might give him warning—
or they might not. Beidermann recalled a time cutting hay when
the smell of smoke was strong in his nostrils, and he tied up his
team to run to the top of the nearby bluff for a look. Unalarmed,
his horses dozed in the cottonwood shade; and presently he

found that he had smelled smoke from an old put-out fire, far off, that no one need worry about anymore. It seemed to him that his horses had known that from the start. . . .

His dogs, however, were as good at warning of fire as they were at everything; it hardly mattered what. Any tiny noise brought the pair of them instantly awake and on their feet; and even anything unheard by Beidermann which somehow intruded on their sleep would cause one eye to slowly open, muzzles elevated a half-inch off the outstretched forelegs; and in one soft movement, a single impulse moving the two, no sound made, they took their full height, their shoulders halfway to Beidermann's hip, and began to pace in a steady pattern, nearer and nearer to Beidermann, their bodies growing stiff if he failed to notice their alarm. But never did they set up the frenzied whining and barking other men admitted their dogs did, as if to boast that such fluster was a mark of quality.

This pair had gone through no fires with him yet, but one of his old man's dogs had, a big old mixed-blood wolfhound that they called Spades because that was what the old man said he was as black as the ace of; the dog following Beidermann and his pony Buster one fall afternoon and chasing whatever they scared up, although there was little life afield in that hot sun. He rode Buster up out of a draw where they had been fooling around in a muddy creek bottom, chasing dragonflies and such, and as the three of them came up the steep side of the ravine onto the gradual slope of the plain, they found themselves square to a line of flame racing out of the northwest.

Just short of panic, young Beidermann started Buster straight east, but smoke lay so thickly around them that they looked to be cut off. Beidermann had heard what to do in such a case; and he laid into Buster until they were mostly free of the smoke, then hauled the pony up and jumped off. From a waxed paper folded in his pocket, he took a match and quickly set a small fire in the scrawniest piece of grass around, hoping it would burn off rapidly, which it did, helped by the same wind that drove the big fire toward them. Beidermann scampered onto the burned-over plot, Buster's reins wrapped around his wrist and hanging on to Spades for dear life. Neither animal, for all the smarts they showed otherwise, was inclined to stay put on this hot and sooty circle, where Beidermann scuffed away an inch or two of hot topsoil, from which tendrils of smoke still rose, to get at cooler depths for them all to stand on. He felt the heat through his boot soles, and he crouched with Spades in his arms, for anytime the dog's paws touched the baked earth he leaped in pain, though never whimpering—the old man wouldn't tolerate a whiny dog. Quickly the fire swept past, not looking all that dangerous from the backside, with foot-high flames and smoke blowing away. But they were safe, and where that vagrant blaze came from and where it went, Beidermann never knew.

When he got home, riding most of the way across the burned-over prairie before reaching the angle where the fire had veered far north, far from the old man's place, he was in such a flurry he could scarcely find words to describe the event. Pa pushed away Spades when he came close, saying: "Now that damn dog's gonna smell like smoke for a month. What business you got out there anyways?"

HE WENT ALONG toward Praeger's but kept looking back. There was nothing to see but the long brown grass slope, although soon in the sky just above the horizon there formed a long, low and thin white cloud. Perhaps not a cloud.

Once more, he pulled the mare around: it wasn't what she had in mind and she fretted. But Beidermann could no longer tell himself that it was no prairie fire down there. It damned well could be, and having admitted that much, he got busy calculating: What did he have for use on it? Not much—no gunnysacks, no shovel, and there was no water down there where the river bowed out nearly three miles.

But what *was* down there he wasn't sure. There might be a touch of water—some old line-camp dugout by a spring; or even a sump well.

Now his own mind wanted satisfying far more than he needed the Praeger boys' work on his flue. He jabbed his heels to the black mare, and she stepped out grudgingly. There was no real smoke to be seen, only that long white cloud, which might be. . . . He told himself that after a mile, two miles, if he saw nothing worse, he'd turn back, ride on to Praeger's with no more than an hour lost.

IT WAS OFTEN A SURPRISE, what came through as clear memory out of the fog of ill feeling he had for his old man. . . . Every night before he turned in, as he stood splay-legged aside the woodpile relieving himself, Beidermann took full and careful measure of the horizon around; the sky nearly always the same slate dome with wispy rainless clouds abounding, and stars like sparkles left by Fourth of July rockets; the horizon even-edged all around except at the jagged span of badlands and the bulge of cottonwoods at the river.

It was exactly the same half-minute's study that his old man had conducted nightly too, when they lived on the north border before Ma died. Young Leo, eight or nine then, watched each night at the time it got fully dark, and the old man, already half asleep, roused himself to go outside, unfastening his britches as he went and with the little finger of his free hand hooking the used-up chaw out of his bottom lip. His narrow eyes peered around under the moon, and Beidermann figured they sought signs of rain, or maybe he cocked an ear for the creaking sound of a late-traveling freighter, whiskey aboard. He never was the kind of man to tell his boy what he hoped for.

Beidermann was eighteen or so, bedding down his own bull trains in the ebony nights and casting his own narrowed eye around to see what was out there, before he realized he was looking for the same thing the old man was.

He thought about it. The old man must have known his neck to bristle a time or two as he watched the midnight horizon grow rosy-fingered, or he wouldn't have been so keen in his nightly look-around. How that worked in a man Beidermann knew more about now: a fellow taking a peaceful leak and on the horizon a dozen miles distant comes a gloomy illumination, changing its shaky shape as smoke dives thick across its front: a sight to block the flow of even such a tough nut as the old man, who knew as well as lesser mortals not to tease disaster with puny bait. . . .

RELUCTANT ENOUGH WHEN BEIDERMANN headed her west, now the black mare turned downright stubborn—a snorting toss of the head, working to grab the bit, a sideways prance when there was nothing spooky in the grass, no snakes, no gopher holes, no grasshoppers even.

This time she picked up the smell of smoke before he did, but he knew what she had found, and it was no surprise. He had only to ride a little farther to see that the thin strands he'd seen a half-hour before from the road here had fattened to lay a mass across the horizon, held in place by a top wind, the smoke whirling side-ways and down, as if seeking to hide until the last moment from snoopers such as Beidermann.

"Goddamn it all to hell," Beidermann yelled, his heart sinking. He prodded the mare forward: she preferred to move sideways, and he dragged her head around with some impatience. He was getting close. The cloud lifted enough to reveal a long line that was its source; it headed far west, maybe across the bow to the river itself. Certainly it was no isolated thistle burn, or haystack or corral fence set afire by Indians disgruntled at another late beef allotment. . . . He hoped to God someone was down there work-ing it, but he saw no sign of that. Himself, he thought, one man, what could he do? Nothing to fight it with . . . His deerskin jacket rested in a roll behind him, but he'd be damned if he'd us that for a gunnysack. There was the mare's heavy saddle blanket, but he'd sure hate to ruin that either. . . .

The fire gave him no good look at itself; only the smoke. He goaded the mare along another half-mile before he caught sight of the flames, although in the bright forenoon sun he saw not flames but the black tips of them, where they turned into smoke. A thin white ash fell.

Now he made out the shape of the fire line. The end of it, near-est to where he came down the slope, popped out of nowhere, boiling from an expanse of charred gray out of which it somehow found grass enough to fuel itself. From that point, it ran far south; Beidermann could not tell how far, but it advanced apace through the abundant blue-stem, which after its springtime fullness had dried to promise fine winter fodder for Schneider's cattle—if this was still his property; somewhere along here ran Krupp's line.

He was close enough now that a little puff of wind sent smoke to envelope him and the mare, to her extreme discomfort. Beidermann cast up and down the line, looking for a gap, a dead spot, where perhaps someone was working; but he saw no one. He had the whole fire to himself.

HIS FIRST PRAIRIE BLAZE had swept down from the northern border through fields of wheat and rye and nearly up to the old man's woodpile, where it furiously burned itself out, stymied by the ground of the yard tamped iron-hard by years of mule traffic. Terrified, Beidermann watched its arrival—the old man being off in Buford or somewhere soaking up the skimpy profits of a summer trapline—and it was nothing he ever forgot. . . . Ever since, that bright wall had flamed at one edge of his consciousness—no particulars, only the idea, the flame. . . .

Among the odds and ends that he remembered from Ma's Bible readings, fire and flood stood out, always menacing . . . fire and brimstone, lakes of fire, fiery pits. Once Ma gave as his lesson the tale of the Seventh Seal. A little of it still stuck:

The fire of the altar was cast into the earth . . . and the third part of all green trees was burnt up, and all green grass was burnt up. . . .

Even in cloudbursts, a part of his mind called up fire, for the lightning could set off a blaze, and if the downpour failed to put it out, it might fester in a rotten oak or cottonwood log waiting until everyone thought themselves safe, when it would shoot up to prove them deadly wrong.

All water reminded him of fire: a flood was no more than God's generous offering to extinguish fire. In the heavy winter storms, with snow banked halfway up his door, central to his mind was the fear of burning out, for the cobs and hay twists stuffed into the cast-iron stove fed a flame that not only warmed Beidermann and his curled-up hounds but heated as well the stick-and-mud chimney, to send it into an internal glow, to set the roof smoldering, all to leap afire when a man fell asleep. He'd seen it happen. . . . And in Skiles, every damned year on the Fourth of July, he saw a fire. Nobody learned. Fireworks everywhere, and then the sudden blaze, the boys with the water-wagon surprised to be called by the gong away from the speeches and pie-eating contests, to gallop to this year's blaze in one vacant lot or another—from which all day earlier had been shagged guilty-looking youngsters, the strings of smoke from their punks trailing behind them as they ran to hide.

THE MARE STILL HAD HOPES of going home. Beidermann bullied her into standing as he watched the line advance. It moved, he judged, about as fast as a healthy baby crawled. Impeded somewhat by the down slope, the wind was not its remorseless self, leaving the fire to set its own pace, and it came forward in measured advance—though at times flashing ahead with a bright orange and black twirl of smoke as it discovered a fat piece of greasewood.

Wiping his smarting eyes with his sleeve, Beidermann considered what stood before him. The fire wanted to come east, where the blue-stem grass grew thickly; and that it seemed to move with little urgency was a delusion, he knew—he could be surrounded in a minute. . . . He found himself reckoning where he could jump in, and what good he could do. But he did have his rifle, and he untied it from beside his leg and fired up a shot, quickly reloaded, and sent off another—for whatever good it might do: someone too far off to see the smoke still might hear. He knew that old Praeger and those tough boys of his would be there soon enough.

It took some muscle now to hold the mare, further unnerved by the shots. Beidermann pointed her east, and she made off in her long-legged lope for a quarter-mile until he drew her up, well above the angle at which the fire seemed headed, and tied the reins to a scraggled sage trunk, anchored well enough to hold her.

Uncinching her saddle, he dragged it clear of the reach of her wild circling, his deerskin coat folded atop. He crammed the damp and heavy saddle blanket under one arm, his rifle under the other to send off additional summoning shots presently, and trotted back to address the line of flames; as the little licks came at him, he whaled away and flattened them to ashes.

The Fourth with Beidermann et Al.

1887

JULY 4. Nary a cloud mars the morning heavens. Were this only another day in a string of hot days in our drouthy summer it would be cause for continued lament, but with the singularity of the occasion, the fierce sun is tolerated; for even as winter's frozen drifts befit celebration of the birth of our Lord Jesus, this bright and shining orb suits our observance of the birth of our Nation. Patriotic weather, sniffs Ma, her garden slowly withering.

It is a steamy journey into Skiles for the celebration, even in the early morning, and necessarily a hasty one, the team set to a cautious trot where the road is good, as we must convey the twins to their recitation by midforenoon, and Ma, finely dressed beside me in the buggy, urges still another hauling forth of my watch for the time; while in back the twins jokingly practice their parts in false acting voices they will not dare to use on stage. Otto has gone ahead, before dawn, as he has duties on the program, and the other boys, August, Cornelius, Harris, promise to come along as they finish their chores; Henry, less of a celebrator, saying he would see.

Now, at the end of the day—and I am not likely to complete this chronicle tonight, but will take it up in the morning for completion—I look back at the events that need telling: there are triumphs; there are surprises; there are satisfactions; there are noisy thrills; there is a drab spectacle or two; there is knowledge imparted slyly; there is sport all around; and there is, of course, contention too, as there will often be when our bachelor neighbor Beidermann shows his face. All in all, even in discord, the Family Praeger participates and does itself proud, most notably through its two youngest members—the twins in their dual recitation, a piece learned during their three-month school term last winter, and their command on stage revealed it as time well spent, as is any time in a school classroom, as I have yet to convince such as Krupp or Schneider, who stubbornly refuse to hire more than a three-month teacher.

We are only in time for the twins' start, and as I tie the team under the box elders with a score of other animals, heads hanging and hides twitching against the flies, the boys race through the crowd to the stage, at the side of which, under a strip of bunting, stands their teacher, Semijahn, beckoning them to hasten and clucking out advice. Quickly to center stage, the boys strike their poses and launch into their dialogue, which is an imaginary one concocted by the clever Semijahn, purporting to take place between William Shakespeare and Gaius Julius Caesar. In it the twins conduct themselves with equal credit, although the preponderance of applause from the hundred-some attending is accorded the Roman; for Professor Semijahn has provided the greater eloquence for the tyrant's utterance, however more suitable it would seem the other way around; but the Bard of Avon suffers an odd lapse of genius on the planks at Skiles: perhaps it is some dark revenge of the Professor's.

The lads receive a rosette and ribbon each from the stern Missus Lovejoy, the banker's wife, and claps on the backs by sundry adults on stage, including old Taubensee, the mayor, who lets others do all the work but never fails to stroll up at the end as if it was all his doing; while the boys' contemporaries hoot from the rear and run off.

Their business over, the twins, relieved, head to the long benches of food in the big tents that Otto and August came in to help raise last week. Franklin Semijahn approaches Ma and me with handshakes and praise for the boys, at their easy skill in declaiming the complex dialogue. He turns aside with a laugh at my query as to how the poet came off second best in his invention.

It is fiction, Mister Praeger, he says and claps me on the back. Dramatic illusion, eh? Heh, heh! But I will tell you, sir, your boys are excellent students. No one would hesitate to call them superior young men.

To be sure, say I. But the Professor has no time to listen to my agreement, as he must hurry away to the day's second main event, the debate, in which he is a participant.

But his suggestion that the twins are fine lads is nothing we have not heard before. I know all my boys well, and the twins are not the only ones superior: there are five others who are so in their own ways, even if they are not revealed in fanciful orations upon a Fourth of July stage. . . .

THE DEBATE WE forgather to hear is put forth thusly: Resolved: The Souls of Persons with Black Skins Are Denied Admission into Heaven, the pro stance adopted by our Professor Semijahn, the con being upheld by the store clerk, Klaus Meirs.

The estimable Meirs has come to Skiles within the past year to keep store, on shares, for Trudell who, having had his fill of trading sugar and spice for eggs and tubs of butter, hard coin never to be seen, retreated to his wife's folks in Ohio, vowing to return when real money could be made. Meirs arrived out of the blue to take over, perhaps a foolish venture, given Schwantz's reputation for giving easy credit. He receives newspapers from both Bismarck and Saint Paul, which he makes available, hung on sticks, to loungers in his store who peruse them with such intensity that each issue is soon in rags; then Meirs holds the tatters at arm's length and twits the readers: How's this? I subscribed to have wallpaper for my bedroom and you have not left me scraps enough to wipe a baby's bottom! He loses money every day.

Now, while youngsters set their fireworks popping afield, their parents sweat in the sparse box elder shade, enrapt in the controversial to-and-fro on stage, and, it soon becomes clear, lend the greater part of their support to the clerk Meirs, for the good reason that his argument ingeniously holds up the Soul as in itself wholly lacking color, whatever the pigmentation of its temporary container—as he calls the skin—of the body it inhabits.

There is no possible answer to his bold call for biblical citation or reference to tenets of known religious doctrines—he excepts Mormonism—that mention the Soul in any color, shade, hue, tincture or pigmentation. Yes, he exclaims, skin surely has properties we arbitrarily call color, but that color does not penetrate to the Soul.

Thus he pins his glib opponent, and the Professor, for all that he argues strenuously, sweating from the brow, fails to produce evidence of how the Soul, itself uncolored, of any black-skinned departed, can possibly be identified with the skin from which it came and for that reason be turned away at the Gate.

The Professor gives it his best try, surely, but even his three cousins in the audience grow lukewarm in their support of his claims that the business happens thusly: no Soul at death can emerge from any body without necessarily taking with it, in ephemeral form, the skin of the body it inhabits—what some people call Ghosts—and wearing it in all its color to Heaven's Gate. But in his struggles to make this clear, the Professor sounds as if he is giving out a recipe for stuffing guts to make sausage; and well-spoken though he is, he delivers his argument in his flapping way, his mouth always open wider than needed to get the words out, as school teachers have a way of doing. When the audience moves in support of his opponent he takes it badly, glaring at us all, and I hope he will not curse us all for fools, as happened in a debate a few years ago with the new Methodist minister from nearby Zimmerman. But the Professor recovers his teacherly equanimity soon enough and, a bit stiffly, gives the clerk Meirs a good-natured pat on the back. He is a great one for slapping people on the back.

OUR MISTER BEIDERMANN IS AT THE PICNIC, come late, it seems.
I glimpse him at a distance with a horse and buggy other than
his own.

That is Anna's buggy, says Ma.

You are wrong there, say I. It is Swede's buggy. And if he
was not dead he would be driving that black gelding and not
Beidermann.

Ma waves her hand impatiently and says nothing.

It is odd to me, seeing Beidermann with horses other than his
big team, those handsome Percherons being the way he makes
his mark amongst us, who are owners of lesser beasts—small-
sized, swaybacked, spiritless animals wearing patched harness—
although today, these horses brought out to trudge in the dusty
procession that Banker Lovejoy calls a gala parade, are groomed
and slicked and wearing their Sunday best blankets or shimmering
fly-nets to conceal sores and disfigurements. Beidermann's champions from last year, in oiled harness and the tinkling bridle bells
of woodland elves, are not to be seen amongst the bunting-draped
wagons and teams hung with ribbons and colored paper twists
braided into manes and tails and driven by embarrassed boys in
top-hat finery, at their sides girls with painted faces holding from
side to side boards adorned with store names—Trudell Mercantile, Schwantz's Mercantile and Fuel, Dakota Saloon and Hotel, all
done in grand looping style by the sign painter, Willy Kuhn. Except for the absence of Beidermann's champions, it is the same as
the past few years. There is the familiar sight of Krupp's big gray
jack, led by Krupp's new hired man, who primps and preens his

way past as if the folks must admire him, who they see for the first time, as much as the mule, which they have seen a dozen times. Indeed, it is an admirable animal, in size, color, conformation, and regal mulish bearing—but in nothing else. It is a worthless animal, although few know this, certainly not those who have passed out blue ribbons to it in parades past. The statuesque beast, for all its apparent muscle, is impossible to work, a biter, a kicker, and will not take a bit. Krupp tries to keep this hidden, but I know, August having witnessed Krupp's adventures with the mule when newly acquired. By August's testimony, the jack, for all its appearance of even temper, undergoes a hideous transformation if shown a harness close up, erupting into such a frenzy of bites and kicks, says August, as would imperil a stout barn wall. Krupp has not managed to teach the worthless beast to tolerate more than a light halter, sufficient to persuade it from one effortless competition to another, as in between it sucks up Krupp's oats and hay at twice the rate of a working animal. Once the desperate Krupp allowed me, with a rueful humor not otherwise shown but required here to forestall open ridicule, that standing for show—as he so grandly put it—is in fact the jack's assigned work. I told him, Then it is the ribbons you should feed that bastard, and not your good oats.

But the big fellow does parade well, following without any show of nerves the band of a dozen out-of-step men tootling their little tin horns and banging their drums like boys at Christmas; whether the plaudits from the roadside are for them or Krupp's mule, it is hard to say.

I see Beidermann's team is not here, then, I say to Ma.

She says, Oh Lord! You do worry too much about him. About him and Anna too, I would say. They came on her buggy, without his team. Stop poking your nose in other people's affairs, for Heaven's sake! You are growing into a snoop, always snooping around him and Anna!

By God, woman! I tell her, peeved. You are the one to talk! I have heard you gossip about those two—

She throws up a hand to cut me off. Women's gossip, she says primly, is not like men's gossip—

Men do not *gossip*, say I. They have no time to sit around and *gossip*—

Hoo! she says. Hogwash, all hogwash, and before you get up on your hind legs and start preaching at me, go get yourself some eats. That potato salad in the blue bowl is mine, and—she rolls her eyes—you will surely want to sample Anna Jenssen's cherry pie.

Before I can say more, she turns and walks off through the grass to a wide cloth awning where Krupp's old lady and some others are selling lemonade for the Methodists. The two skinny Jenssen girls are washing cups, and I stretch to see if the Widow herself is amongst the jumble of long skirts and bonnets behind the planks set on sawhorses to hold the tubs in which jugs of lemonade float half-tipped. She is not to be seen, but Ma catches me looking and throws up her hands to tell me I am hopeless.

Schneider's oldest boy is selling fireworks off his wagon, as he is the enterprising sort who would do so. He is within a year or two of Harris's age; a big, red-haired bouncing fellow, where Harris' feet never leave the ground, unless he is wrestling someone to the death. To attract attention to his wagon he whirls a silvery pinwheel over his head and whistles as if calling hogs while holding up a fistful of firecrackers in their colorful Chinese paper.

What price are you asking? say I.

He has a whole array, and holds up this, that and the other; and tosses off prices. This is a cent, this is two cents, this ladyfinger is two for a cent, this is two for a nickel; all these big ones are a dime apiece—they make one Hell of a noise, believe me.

On both his arms the red hair is singed away. Around him, on the wagon bed, his colorful display is like a picture from an Oriental art book.

He says, They all come from Saint Paul, and they cost a pretty penny too. You have to mail off your order before Easter and send all the money too, and then the company ships them on the railroad.

I might buy a few, say I, if it does not break the bank.

I take a double handful of the two-for-a-penny and, pocketing those, select two of the ten-cent size, which the Schneider boy gives me, saying, Yessir, you can blow up a bank with those, as I store them in my vest, and call the twins from the horseshoe pits. They have shot the fireworks Ma gave them, which she had somehow saved from last year; and I hand over my supply of the two-for-a-pennies as they whoop and dash in search of the boy with the punk. With two fat cylinders in my pocket I feel cunning indeed, although I have no intention for their use—unless, for a little fun, I light one under Krupp's regal jack.

Ma is at the vat of floating watermelons, slicing wedges for the children running up, as I remind her that speech-time is drawing near; and I stroll off through friends and neighbors, all with pleasant words for one another, to find a shady spot before the stage, empty except for the play of small children since the Black Souls debate. Upon it now, doing his annual stint, comes little

Willy Kuhn, the sign-painter from Zimmerman who makes Skiles his second home as he courts—into the third year now—the hefty Vogel girl. Befitting his trade, he has an artistic or actorly bent, and yodels like an auctioneer for us all to step up, and slaps at the low-hanging bunting as he does a little side-step dance, daintily, onto the stage center, his foot-tall red, white, and blue hat wobbling so that he must hold it in place, yelling that this is the main event, step up, step up; for all that everyone interested in speeches is already in place. In case there is a straggler, Willy Kuhn waits a decent time, and then begins his introduction of the man—he says the same for every speaker—who needs no introduction; as always the first speaker, the banker Dewey Lovejoy.

Over the top of his round spectacles the banker studies us severely, as if searching for anyone delinquent in his payments, and he clears his throat disgustingly several times before grumbling into his speech. First he mentions the hard times come to test honest folk, and he seems to include himself in those being tested, for all that he lives fat. Hard times, he says, must be met forthrightly, by honest folk, stoically, without whining or complaint, always making payments on time. No weaklings needed here, he says, patting his paunch. But we should not look just at ourselves, he cautions, as there is a great country abuilding. Banker Lovejoy would beg that we regard the thrust of history, with particular attention to how financial investments have influenced its path, as even our ancestors made their payments on time, a legacy not to be dishonored. The more he talks, the more it sounds as if higher interest rates on his loans are forthcoming.

He is at least brief—having nothing in his head to say unless it promises money for his bank—unlike the windbag Puckett, fetched now to the stage by Willy Kuhn with an introduction that makes the wispy, bald little fellow sound like Moses on a special visitation to Dakota. As the assistant to the Territorial Congressional delegate, Bouchard Clausen, he is filled to overflowing with news of Clausen's heroic efforts on our behalf in Washington. For all that any evidence of which he speaks remains unseen, and his vague talk of lower tariffs sounds nonsensical, coming as it does after Lovejoy's equally vague talk of higher interest; but his words are attended to politely, as he is our official link to Eastern power.

Well, I think he is honest, says Ma, having come up beside me.

You need not worry about him, say I. He is small potatoes. Worry about that boss of his nobody has ever seen.

Now, behind Willy Kuhn's strident summons, Karl Deitrich, retired land agent and prominent war veteran, steps to the plank to deliver his annual rouser, distilled from his supposed experiences in the Union Army, although I would be unsurprised to learn that our Karl was a bugler boy and not the confidant of colonels as he makes himself out. Still, no one can deny he has a way, a loud and hearty way, of shouting forth his various slogans, that include FREEDOM! LIBERTY! A GREAT PEOPLE! A CHRISTIAN NATION! &tc., &tc., which make no sense if used as normal people use words every day, but he drums up such a marvelous roar in his bass voice that it stirs the lot of us into a mighty cheer, and he is encouraged to go on: YEOMAN OF THE PLOW! HEARTY PIONEERS! &tc. . . .

Regularly, three or four a minute, throughout the speeches, comes the pop of fireworks, sometimes followed by an angry shout. A few dogs which the owners have allowed to follow their wagons into town cower under them now. But not—I see, just beyond the livery barn—Beidermann's rapacious hounds, their owner nowhere in sight. Far from cringing at the fireworks, his dogs lay unflinching, though panting heavily in the heat. Notable beasts they are, not only for their size but for their coloration, which is a patchwork of black and brown, the drab colors blending into each other across their backs and sides, so that they look made of mud and road dirt. They are tied with rope to the under-carriage of Swede's buckboard, which brought Beidermann, the Widow, and her daughters into town, and in the small shade the seat casts they stretch on their bellies, long and limber forelegs laid neatly to the front, and dark tongues pulsing at full length. They need water, surely, although I am not the man to succor them, having been given opportunity to examine their angrily bared fangs at close range for no reason other than stepping off my rig too near Beidermann's barn door. They are not bashful animals; they take what they want and all else tear up and let rot.

Now the twins trot near, smudged of face and hand, fleeing some distant commotion, a fair quantity of fireworks still in their clutch, and when I point out Beidermann's thirsty hounds, they run to fetch melted ice dipped from the lemonade tubs into a cake-tin snatched from beneath the bench.

Given water, the dogs unfold their lengthy legs and greet the lads as if they are Beidermann himself: another benefactor would be greeted less cordially. I have seen recent evidence of their savagery: by the river where the twins, fishing, called me to see a small doe, legs torn off whole, her ass-end wholly chewed away, and her throat gone too. They are no better than wolves, these creatures Beidermann dotes upon, killer dogs, sure enough. I watch them slop up the water as the twins run off. Over the years I have shot a few of their kind who found their way too close to my cattle, and they ended their days nailed to a stump, to let the owners of others with a like propensity know where they can look for hounds left to run amongst my stock: nailed by the ears to the nearest cottonwood, by God.

Some part of the audience has dribbled away as each speaker finishes, although none turns away from Banker Lovejoy's threats and warnings, for fear he will notice and remember and perform one of his famous foreclosures, for all that the bank already has taken over more land than it can oversee.

Now there are two score people left with Ma and me: August, having avoided banker and politician, comes up as Deitrich winds down: perhaps the boy hopes to draw a bit of cheer and optimism from the patriot's bombast. THIS HAPPY BREED! OUR STALWART KIND! But clearly he is running out of steam, and the audience is ready for the horse race soon to start at the south end of town, and the three-legged gunnysack races, and the endless egg-throw contest, going on to the north.

August, standing between Ma and me, says, Did you give the twins that bunch of fireworks?

I did, say I.

You did? says Ma. I did.

You gave them the ones you hid from them last year, say I. I gave them some from this year.

She frowns. How many do they need? she asks crossly.

August, doubtless sorry he has asked his question, draws back. On stage, Deitrich seeks a thundering conclusion, and he pulls off his stained gray derby, pretending that in his exuberance he will fling it into the midst of his few remaining listeners. A look of apoplexy is upon him. GALLANT SODBUSTERS! BRAVE VISIONARIES! HARBINGERS OF FORTUNE! &tc.

Old Deitrich, I say to Ma, begins to sound like chapter titles in a school book—

Yaaas, he surely does.

This is not Ma's voice. It is Beidermann, who leans in between Ma and me, and speaks loudly, above the claps of a half-dozen people relieved that Deitrich finishes short of seizure.

Aha! say I. So here you are. I saw your dogs, left without water. We missed your horses in the parade. He is nicely dressed in a blue striped shirt and brown vest and britches, and expensive-seeming new boots, or old ones well polished up.

Did you? he says absently, as if this is of no interest to him. But he pokes a thumb into my arm. Have you been listening to these boys' speeches? says he, and goes on without waiting for my answer: Let me ask you something: it gets worse every year, does it not? Everybody giving themselves a pat on the back, telling each other how worthy they are. That old boy with the army sash must have been hit in the head with a cannon ball—

Ma speaks up sharply. He has been through a lot, she says. And he has a right to make his feelings heard.

Beidermann hesitates, as if he is reluctant to argue with a woman, and he turns his shoulder toward her. Now, behind the food tents, the pits of open coals are ready and slabs of beef laid down, and ropes of smoke with enticing odors drift our way. Around us, everyone heads in that direction. On stage Kuhn presents the ribbon for largest family at the fair to old Meyerhoff, who has increased his brood to fourteen since taking the award last year. Beidermann leans down to speak to me, quietly, as if he hopes Ma will politely not listen.

All these pats on the back, says Beidermann, I fail to understand it. This whole crew here, none of 'em at all, did a thing to take personal credit for. They aint done a thing themselves. Misfits and failures, went bust in the East; come crawling out here from New York or Pennsylvania, their grandpas did, and maybe got as far as Illinois or Wisconsin, and went bust there too, and now these old boys, looking for a dollar in the road, turn up in Dakota scratching s--t with the sparrows, and get up on the stage and pat themselves on the back. By God!

The critical Beidermann, I am reminded, comes not from the East, but down from the North, so may grandly exempt himself from those of us of Eastern ancestry.

All failures, says Beidermann. Shiftless ones, drunken ne'er-do-wells, dull ones and stupid ones, too scared or foolish to make a go of it back there. Some of 'em could not tie a knot, fell over their own feet when they went to turn around; but kept coming west, they did, until they got far enough west so they could pat themselves on the back and now they tell each other how great they are just for having sense enough to put one foot in front of another until they got here. Hell, some of 'em are even criminals, running from the law—

Well, Beidermann, say I, it may be you are speaking of your own ancestors, but as for mine—

By God, but it rubs me wrong, he says, folks taking credit for nothing. Look at the bunch of them—he waves his hand to take in the town—congratulating themselves for being forced further and further West, pushed back like the runt pig to the last shriveled tit that gives no milk.

Come, come, Beidermann, say I. This is a picnic celebration, and if this is your Fourth of July antidote speech, well, there are no anarchists here to appreciate it—

Yeoman of the plow! cries Beidermann. Christ, Praeger, you know as well as I do, next Fourth, one-third of the people here will be bust, and they will not even be sucking the sow's hind tit, they will be begging off the wife's folks back East. No wonder that oily banker is so suspicious about lending money—hardly anybody here knows enough to make a crop to bring in enough money to pay it back. Hell, they go and put ten cows on land that can not feed one—and they pat themselves on the back—

August, at my side, now gives a loud laugh like a cough. Well, says he, I guess what you mean by all this bulls--t is that while us poor folks are sucking hind tit, you got yourself that rich bottom land and all that good hay so you are sucking *front* tit, eh? He smiles at Beidermann, mildly enough.

Beidermann peers around me, as if August's insignificant presence had gone unnoticed until this interruption. Now he throws back his head, enabling him to look down that great Roman nose, and with a little smile, says at last: You, being a Praeger boy, would recognize bulls--t when you see it, as you are all so full of it yourselves.

Between the two, I stand with a hand on August's elbow. These are sour words from Beidermann, and no surprise as he is a man given to them, but for all their familiarity, no easier to swallow. And yet he is our neighbor, our closest neighbor; the twins spend near as much time at his place as they do at ours. And if he is unconcerned with the possible grievous consequences of such unneighborly utterances, I am not. But I push my concerns aside, for I have seen the ugly aftermath of radical words exchanged between neighbors. All of us here, we Yeoman of the Plow have seen our fill of such consequences: men and boys dead, dogs poisoned, hay and barns burned: and this last spring, young Duycinck's remains found afloat in the willows of the flooded Sheyenne below Fort Eden; flung into the icy flood I have no doubt by . . . someone . . . whose name will be revealed in good time, and he will prove to be a good neighbor of Duycinck, the two having argued over fence lines and so-called trespass. And this . . . someone . . . is a civilized man, educated at an Eastern university; but now in the end to be counted as one of Beidermann's Eastern failures of the outlaw persuasion; for while this gentleman is clever at making his way, never bankrupt, meeting all payments, neither shiftless nor without good luck, yet he is fated soon to wear a hempen necktie. . . .

But August has heard Beidermann's vaporish rants before, and I will give my boy this: he has a sweet nature, for without rancor he replies to Beidermann's aspersion: I mean only that you have no right to call people failures who have had nothing but bad luck, with drouth and storms and fires. Anybody can get behind when those things happen, and if they live through them, then a pat on the back is nothing wrong. You have had uncommon good luck. Others have not.

He speaks forthrightly, uncontentious in manner; and I would say, of the seven boys—counting even the twins, who are half August's age—all will provoke a fight without half trying: only

August turns away ire with a wry smile, a mild word, a dismissing wave of the hand. The boy has courage enough, but feels little need for its reckless display.

Now Ma pushes past August and me and squarely eyes the stiff-necked Beidermann. Leo, says she into his face, Leo, you are nothing but a preacher who no one would ever give a pulpit to. You want us all to admit how worthless we are—in your eyes if not in the eye of God—and then you will show us mercy in saving us from our terrible sins. Well, we cannot all be perfect like you. Take my advice, Leo, and get yourself a church and leave people alone to have a good time on the Fourth.

Stock still, Beidermann takes this in with squinted eyes and a small smile, but before Ma finishes suddenly he jumps as if tweaked in the hinder and cranes to see over my shoulder as behind me a long shout is raised, and Beidermann pushes past, running.

Without turning to look I can tell anyone who asks what it is: the dependable event without which the Fourth would not be the Fourth: another damn grass fire.

The fleet Beidermann is already across the road as August and I hasten after, a flurry of men beside us, to the large weedy lot between the livery and Schwantz's store, above which a half-dozen ribbons of smoke spiral into the hot sky; no one needing to be told that fireworks have set alight the dry growth there, upon which a swarm of men with shovels and gunny sacks have descended, and as I come up Beidermann is dancing on the last of the sparks at the edge of a charred spot two rods each way.

Beyond the stomping Beidermann I see three boys high-tailing it out of town, no doubt hoping to outrun the paternal switch.

The twins, coming up, announce that these are the Anderson boys, who are a jolly trio, full of clever riddles—I have heard them stump the twins—and sly jokes, but always more innocent ones than the setting off of fires, for all that it is an accident.

From the burned lot, Otto emerges bearing a shovel with which he knocks charred weeds off his boots. The shovel he returns to old Arno Gaustad, who stands under the flag pole at the post office as if he is keeper of the colors, which hang limply above his head.

Good there is no wind, he says, with stiffened fingers tying the shovel to the side of his grandson's wagon from whence it came, Otto having wrested it away to forestall him, limping and wheezing, from doing battle with the fire himself. However fit he looks and claims himself to be, at eighty-some years a man cannot jump around fighting fires without encouraging the Almighty to express His awful disapproval. Old Gaustad stays close to his grandson's wagon, which is just as well, a horse being too much for him to ride these days; but there are years upon which he left his mark—and which left their mark upon him, namely, the skinned patch on the back of his head, where hair never properly grew again for all his years of trying, after a slab of skin the size of a lady's hand was pulled clear off by a she-wolf into whose den the young Gaustad crawled halfway, thinking it empty. The terror-crazed animal soon clawed her way out over his back in a space big enough only for one of them—who was scared most we do not know—but her escape came at the expense of a little of his skin and scalp. He was just married then, and when he turned up at home bloody from head to toe, his wife surely had doubts as to the sort of fool she had picked herself.

From that misadventure old Gaustad forever bears scars, but he has lived amongst us since as a dignified man, with a fading reputation as one bold enough to poke his bare head into a wolf's den. His little fringe beard, now purely white, is neatly trimmed, by his wife, no doubt, if she can still see to do it, or perhaps by his daughter Ida, who married a Taubensee, whose son has fetched the lot of them to the picnic.

Old Gaustad's wife has claimed a straight-backed wooden chair by the watermelon tub, to keep count on those who come around for extra slices, swatting fearlessly at the paper wasps and bees come to sample the cut melons. One clouded eye she keeps peeled on her grandson's wagon, now to see that the old man ties up the shovel properly. She calls him on any job done not to her liking; I have seen it. She has definite likes. She sits here without spectacles, although surely she wears them at other times, but is too vain to present herself in eyeglasses at public events; for all that she wears a faded wash bonnet.

I think it has been last Fourth since I saw Gaustad; his place, his children's places, and his grandchildren's places being too far north for us to meet often. When he has twice tested the knots securing the shovel, I approach to shake his hand, and he confirms, yes, it was the last Fourth that we laid eyes on one another.

By God, say I, to humor him, you have a better memory of that than I do.

Well, why not? says he. I am a hell of a lot better looking too!

He is not hard of hearing, and he tells me he gets around fairly good. His grandson, he tells me first off, has planted rye on a big spread added by purchase of a quarter-section from some Irishman who has returned to his wife's folks in Indiana after one bad dry year; he tells this not to scoff at the unlucky Irishman, but to point out that not one dry year, nor two, nor three, has done in the two of us; although that is not his news: the planting of so much rye is.

I suppose you heard those speeches, I say.

I heard 'em all right, says Gaustad. I heard that Goddamned banker. I like to hear bankers talk. Some people do not, but I do. They always talk money, even when they talk something else. You listen close, you will find out something about your own money—that is, providing you got any. They know a lot about money that you and me never thought of.

There may be something to that, say I.

You damned right. Banker knows what a dollar means. To you and me a dollar means a mess of flour and sugar and beans, some coal oil, that sort of thing. Hell, that aint what it means to a banker. What one dollar means to him is *another* dollar—you damned right! If he has got one, he is bound and determined to make it two. One aint enough! Are you the kind of fellow who thinks like that? I sure aint.

No, I am surely not, say I.

Let me tell you something else, Gaustad says, peering up into my face. I like that old boy Karl Deitrich too. He knows how to get up a head of steam. He should have been a politician. Or a preacher. He would have made a good preacher—get the unbelievers to their knees straightaway. I know he was a sh--y land agent, but hell, he should have been a preacher. If he preached for the Methodists, I might go hear him.

Arno, say I, I ought to get Beidermann over here to talk to you. Who is that?

Beidermann, fellow moved in south of me a couple years back.

The fellow with the team of big blacks? I know who he is. What about him?

Well, he thinks different—

S--t, lots of people think different, the whole world thinks different. The hell with 'em. I know what I think, and I lived longer than any of 'em.

There is a wailing at his knees which comes from three of old Gaustad's great-grandchildren, hauled up here by his grandson, all three crabby at being pulled away from the unfinished festivities, the pie-eating contest in particular; the grandson, the seat of his trousers stained with dirt and grass from his having been pulled down on the losing side in tug-of-war, waves to Grandma at the melons to get moving; they must leave. They have as long a ride home as anyone here, and had they left an hour earlier, it would still be dark by the time they reach their place; all chores to be done in lantern light: and so the two boys and little girl are sullen, close to tears in this cheery sunlight, fireworks popping, knowing they will fall unhappily asleep in the jarring wagon, to be wakened in the dark and sent to do the milking in the dismal barn, while the alarmed cows throw their heads about to see why they are being tended so late, in the shadows.

I know how that is, coming home in the dark, but it is our luxury that the Family Praeger need not hasten unduly, as the sober sided Henry, who, as he says, in thirty-two years has far and away had his fill of the dust and noise and foolish speechifying called the Fourth, stays home, probably reading, and does the necessary chores: feeding the calves and hogs, bringing in the bull, closing up the chickens; and we will find him with his history of Athens and Sparta and all that beside the kitchen lamp when we come up the dark lane under the stars.

JULY 5. As I finish up yesterday's chronicle in the heat of this morning, Ma comes to my desk holding the two cylinders of fireworks found in my vest; they are bigger around than my thumb and with their hen scratch printing look very foreign in her hand.

What is your purpose in saving these? she says.

I will ask you a question too, say I. What is your purpose in poking through my pockets?

She does not answer that, but says, These look like something a person would use at a shivaree. She sets them at my hand and goes to leave.

Wait, wait, say I. What was the gossip over those watermelons, then? About Beidermann and the Widow, was it? Tying the knot, are they?

Women's gossip, she says. I know you are not one to believe women's gossip. Going out the door she says over her shoulder, But save those silly fireworks of yours, all the same.

Beidermann and
the Hard Words

✥

⊷ 1887 ⊷

AUG. 2. An over-heated wind all day, and the dust that rides on it—not simple dust but dirt itself, the Earth itself. The rags Ma stuffs in door and window sills hold back only some; and grit in her kitchen, on the oil-cloth, pots, in the water-pail, a skin of it everywhere, near gives her fits. With grit in our teeth, we spit black.

That wind is too much to work in for more than a few hours, in that the horses will stand tail to it, heads lowered and eyes hooded, tails blowing back across their rears. Among us it goes unsaid, though bursting to be said, there will be little crop any-where this season in this part of Dakota; except in the small greener bottoms of the river where, for all that the heat goes as it does everywhere, yet the baking wind is less. Those fields are the lucky Beidermann's, indeed, the blessed Beidermann's, for it is as if the drouth chooses to pass him by; his good fortune being that the greater part of his land lies where the river still shows something more than a damp stain; at which our cattle contend with his along its snaking length, a hundred heads tossing and tails whipping against the flies that cover them like a coat of blacking wherever mud is not crusted, as it is on their legs and underbellies, baked there like armor-plating. Today, the twins peel off sheets of it from a skinny heifer before she summons strength enough to stagger free.

AUG. 3. God gives no quarter, sending nary a cloud, nor one the size of a baby's hand, against the fearsome sun, which shortly murders any beneath it that turn for a moment careless. Henry, coming home from the north section with the hides off two calves gone under from this onslaught, rides in himself dizzied and half-addled; and here it is well into the still-hot night and he has watered himself thoroughly, inside and out, and only now does he come weakly into my lamp's light, and sighing heavily takes a little of the meat and potato Ma left out for him.

AUG. 4. Even as he stands and watches, vows Otto, he can discern the measure of decline of the water in our well. It is nearly so; against the fading wetness of the stone wall, it descends the width of a girl's finger each day; and the rope paid out today to fetch a bucketful exceeds by my arm's length the amount required to do the job after the spring thaw. Much of what we take from it goes to keep Ma's garden decent; and she begrudges more of it than I would to her damned geraniums, which flaunt their health while the grass six feet from them is dead, and the leaves on the box elder by the porch are gray, not green.

The twins return late from a day helping Beidermann scrape up a dam at a trickle of a spring he has lately, most providentially, discovered, and they report the pool sufficient to provide the stock consigned thereabouts; even as Beidermann's home-place well, which they assisted in digging, is no less full than when they dug it, say they; and they express puzzlement, then, why our own should drop, as if there is some flaw in my placement of it, done before they or any of the boys, excepting Otto, were even born; but my explanation that our bachelor neighbor draws from a different reserve, appears to fade away unheard. There is this too, left unsaid, for it would seem sour: that Beidermann's good fortune does not waver much, however the destinies of others are jarred and twisted as God sees fit to do so often; and if such blessings result from our staunch neighbor's close attention to his land and animals, why, then, those of us who labor no less strenuously have cause to ponder how even-handedly the destinies of men on Earth are administered from on High, and to ask in a whisper behind closed doors, whether some are not being dealt a shorter hand than others.

AUG. 8. Beidermann arrives today for the loan of our rake, as if to impress upon us that he has hay to use it on while we do not. His massive team is in empty harness, himself astride the mare, and swinging off that broad back, he says: I come along the bluff to the south, and I see your stock there are mostly skin and bones. God-damn this heat!

You have that wrong, say I. God is not likely to damn it, as it is Him who sends it.

From under the wide brim of his cloth hat, Beidermann's cool squint rests upon me. Another time he might laugh. The two of us have had our words before on Providence and the workings of Nature, and Mister Beidermann makes it clear that he sets no store in help nor hindrance by way of Heaven.

So you have the right to think, says our philosopher neighbor, but I will tell you this: it is just a turn of the big wheel we are up against, and when it turns more we will get better times. There are rewards due us all.

Yes, say I. Rewards in the Hereafter . . . and I ask you, sir, who is it that spins that big wheel of yours?

As always, Beidermann has his answer ready: From the looks of your animals, I would say it is the Devil, eh, boys? He nods to the twins with a wink; and the two of them look to me, reluctant to say: Beidermann is right, look at how he prospers. I know that in the several years spent at his heels they have been persuaded by the able Beidermann and his ways; in this easy trust being the very opposite of my older boys, who stand warily aside and watch.

Beidermann backs his team over the rake's tongue and says: If I get two-thirds of what I made last year, I will count myself a lucky man.

Count yourself that, then, say I, for I have not put up nearly half a crop, and there is nothing for another cutting.

Beidermann grunts, a half-angry sound that means no commiseration with my lot, but is instead a noise of displeasure at his unturning wheel, that it is stuck in this rut.

. . .

AUG. 10.

We dropped the seed o'er the hill and plain
Beneath the sun of May. . . .

It is now the sun of August and another story, for the wheat we have seen so far is all we shall see: a stunted lot, indeed, not half-grown, kernels small as lice and hard as stone, and we will cut it for straw for want of another choice; Otto sensibly declaring that it is a few weeks' winter fodder not otherwise come by and which we will badly need: and there is abundant time to carry out the bleak reaping chore, for we are freed from all labor of a normal harvest in this sun-struck country: among us all, only Beidermann needs extra hands to put up his so-called two-thirds. Cornelius and the twins will take a team and rack over; and doubtless he also has the exchange of help from Krupp and all the others as well. . . .

AUG. 11. Ma looks over my shoulder just now, having read her night's piece, this from the book of Jeremiah, that I must hear. He tells us, says Ma, that we are brought

to a plentiful country to eat the fruit thereof, but now we have forsaken
the fountain of living waters, and hewed out cisterns, broken cisterns,
that can hold no water; and then, we hast polluted the land with our
whoredoms and wickedness. Therefore the showers have been with-
holden and there hath been no latter rain.

Well, Ma, say I, that is Jeremiah and this is us. But it is something to chew on, all right. There is no question about the broken cisterns and no rain—but what is this whoredom and wickedness? Unless we have been missing something big, the only thing that comes close to that in this country is Beidermann and the Widow Jenssen.

Oh, shhh, says Ma, piqued. It is not them. It is the sinfulness of us all.

That may be so, say I, and Beidermann is sure one of the sinners, but still his cistern did not break, did it?

AUG. 12. Henry reports that Krupp, whom he encounters on the west section setting out poison baits for a prairie wolf he thinks chewed up one of his calves, now favors us with rumors of grasshoppers twenty miles south of Skiles. But that is Krupp; and these are rumors in a country where hope goes under often, so that a man learns to expect disaster: as a full moon is certain in its time, so is Krupp known to adumbrate catastrophe: when matters are grim, they will grow worse before getting better; it will become hotter before it cools; drier before it rains; colder before it warms; a deeper freeze before thaw; hail before harvest, &tc., &tc.—the promise of calamity swiftly seen, so that one's guard may be raised against even harder times, and the heart prepare itself to bear the harder event, which is sure to occur. . . .

But as for Krupp's grasshoppers we must wait and see, although without happy anticipation. I have seen them more than once, and it is another kind of world they bring. Fire is no worse, for flames can be fought and sometimes quelled.

But we shall see. It is thus every August—rumors of the dread plague. So has it been since Biblical times when it was the dread locust; which old Gaustad calls them still—locusts; as if he can, in all his tottering years, remember them from that very time.

AUG. 14. What is it we are meant to do, then? The sun will soon take all. The hot wind punishes without a moment's surcease. We all grow uglier, nor do we give a thought to it that we do. Otto, the oldest, always steadfast, comes from the dinner table, turns on the porch step, and abruptly vows that he will leave this God-damned place, saying he should have done so long ago, it being an unfit place for white men; and here he has wasted a life of thirty-five years upon it. . . . And for all that there is the land that I chose— while not my first choice, given the railroad's gluttony, but my choice still—Otto in his torment puts my judgment into question, although I feel no call to answer, for the boy has no malice in him; it is all despair.

But it is something other than despair in his younger brother, Harris; who shows such a constant agitation of discontent, barely contained, that his own mother, with her heart open to all her seven sons equally, looks on him with doubts, as if he is visited upon us as a family test, with his cruel, black moods and sour way overall.

Now he mocks Otto, saying: Oh, yes, maybe you should pull out for the sand country, where all the pickings are rich, eh? Cook yourself up a nice batch of burrs and nettles for your supper, eh?

Long past taking issue with his peevish brother, Otto says: Only a God-damned fool would try to hang on here year after year. . . . He adds bitterly: And it looks like I am one of them.

But I know that among them all he is one who will not go, for as the poet knows,

Not what we would, but what we must,
Makes up the sum of living. . . .

AUG. 15. In the creek in our north pasture—but there is no creek: tiny, bitter pools, a trickle sometimes, the foul water insufficient for a man to wash his feet. This, reports Henry, as if he has come up with some jarring news, is the worst he has ever seen it.

For some, any new affliction is the worst. I have seen it worse.

AUG. 16. The twins report that the busy Beidermann has cut a good crop of hay off his most southern acreage, so good that he has traded a portion of it to Reinhardt for a hog, which the old man cannot feed, but Beidermann can. . . . Our Beidermann does his business as if conditions of the drouth impose no more hardship on him than would any sunny day, and therefore the rest of us, in our complaining, are spineless as chickens: surely, this rubs the most easy-going among us the wrong way. For me, or Krupp, or Reinhardt, this Beidermann is little more than a visitor: hardly five seasons in this territory—whatever part of the world he has graced in his undisclosed past—so his high-horse manner cannot derive from special knowledge of what prevails here, among us, for he is innocent of that. . . . How many others have I seen set themselves up in full confidence one year, and the next, when from sun or fire, hail or storm, for all that man and wife and every child works dawn to dusk, they get so far behind that they must crawl with their tails between their legs back to the wife's folks back East? I can hardly count their number.

And still Beidermann does more than well, given these grim times, where the rest of us do not, as if such lordly assurance generates its own success, even at a time when failure is in the wind itself; and if that wind bears the rumored grasshoppers to us, it is more than failure and even the valiant Beidermann's certitude will shrink to the size of a grain of my wheat.

AUG. 17. Early, the day has some body to it, but with the rising of the sun, there is only the singular dimension of Old Sol. Heat, heat, and more of it; the air is thinned by it and even the wind lacks heft; so that two breaths are needed to do the work of one; and birds flying through seem weakly borne, though few birds fly: a single crow flaps high, another soon follows, both silent where usually they are the noisiest of creatures.

AUG. 18. So, it is no rumor but a prophecy—or possibly a grand prank, that grasshoppers come in a season where there is so little for them to destroy: but come they do, in dread abundance. . . . At noon, August hastens across the yard and calls through the screen door in the porch where I am washing up for dinner: They are here!

Over his shoulder in the western sky comes one small, dark cloud, their cruel vanguard; which as I watch twists somewhat to the north to reveal broadside the tail of itself; that small cloud being only the head of a long stream in the shape of a great tadpole, rising up from some hidden place, miles off, while its tail reaches to the horizon.

They are headed more north, I say.

No, says August. You are fooling yourself. They are coming to us, for certain.

His words are their invitation. That thickening cloud swerves again, enlarging itself somehow, once, twice. Ma, coming to the door, quilts in hand, cries: Cover the garden! They will have it all!

It is little enough, her garden, but the last healthy green left for us to look on.

With what? says August. Those quilts? What is it they will not eat?

My prayer is that they will still pass us by, at least in the main; but I hasten to the shed, August following, and the twins coming up on their ponies, from wherever they have been, and Otto and Cornelius coming from the barn; and from the shed we drag forth the cowhides stored there.

They will eat these, too, says Otto, flattening bean vines, to lay the stiff hides across; but we cover what we can, while Ma spreads her quilts over her geraniums and the new strawberry plants.

The first of our visitors descend, no more than we might see on a normal summer's day. They gaily leap, not so much flying as gliding for great distance: another leap, another glide. But behind these few scouts, the cloud unfolds, expands, becomes black as prairie smoke, as massive as the throngs of pigeons I have seen back East, spreads itself down on us; a crashing deluge, like buckets of hail crackling down. We have not finished tying cords around our sleeves and pants cuffs before they seethe over us, clinging for an instant and dropping away. The cowhides go thick with them, in overlapping layers, those on top covering those beneath, and another layer smothering those. Ma's quilts seem to change colors as the insects swarm across.

The twins, in awe and amazement, seeing this phenomenon for the first time with other than infant eyes, cease work and stand staring at the mounds crawling at their feet, and kick at them; until Ma calls and they run, looking back at the sheet of insects settling at their heels, to the kitchen to help her renew her rag seals around windows and doors.

Around my legs the chickens flutter and hop with whimpering chirps, startled by the thin, dry buzz all around; and all the while peck away in a frenzy, scarcely moving from one spot, engorging themselves.

At the barn, Cornelius hollers for help to haul in the harness left draped on the fence, before it is eaten; the sweat-salted collars and breeching already clotted to double their size with the thronging insects: Cornelius scrapes them away in handfuls as he drags the harness to the safety of the barn; and they are thick as snow about my face as I go to help him: a crisp sting as one strikes skin, clinging until knocked away to make room for another; and a carpet of them underfoot—dozens crushed with the sound of crusted snow beneath each footfall.

From the barn door, above the windy sound of the besieging creatures, I hear the swine set up a contented snuffling as they suck up their rich supper in slobbering mouthfuls, hardly moving their long snouts to take up another pintful, so thickly do the insects clog their trough.

And still there come more, although there is no room for more. Miles away west, a new wide sheen veers across the horizon, nearing us; the sun glints on the membranes of their wings; a jewel-like sparkle all throughout their mass. The newcomers tumble in fist-sized lumps onto their brothers already thickly here, locust upon locust, a half-dozen deep, now a dozen, as if they would eat through each other to get at the ground beneath that is already gnawed bare. By the chicken coop, they come up to the hens' thighs; some of the fowls already so overstuffed they can barely move; and some foolish ones, filled to bursting, with beaks open gasp for air as they squat and tip to their sides: some are goners, and given time to butcher them now, before their feathers are chewed away and their meat polluted, they will be edible; but by tomorrow the tenderest portions of their flesh, having absorbed what they eat today, will taste vile.

I have forgotten the horses: I call to Otto, and he waves a hand toward the upper pasture where they stand nervously in a turning string, looking back with heads high; then their hind-ends swivel about and they look again. . . . Out in the pasture there are no birds. Where are the birds that rescued the Mormons? Every lark, every robin, every bold crow, is gone to hide. . . .

AUG. 19. Midmorning, as the twins and Cornelius and Henry and I caulk the walls of the barn loft with dampened rags, that we might preserve such hay as we have rescued from the weather, I hear Henry mutter and I look up to see a wagon coming up our road through shallow drifts of grasshoppers; and if I did not recognize Beidermann, I would know his handsome team.

The Great Man cometh, says Henry.

The twins run ahead, batting grasshoppers left and right from their faces: no less beleaguered, I come out of the barn as Beidermann pulls up his grand Percherons, which stand unsure against the invading insects, planting and unplanting each plate-sized hoof and killing grasshoppers each time; ears and eyes atwitch, hides shivering.

Beidermann gives me a sprightly hallo. I will tell you something, he says. These sons of bitches will eat anything. Look here.

He lifts the mare's right front leg and runs the dirty fetlock through his fingers. Look! he says. They et it! Et the God-damned hair, they did. They will eat the hide right off your animals, you bet!

To my eye, the hair, dirty and ragged as it would naturally be, could have been chewed on or could not have been—there was no telling. But his horses stood like set-out meals here, and I sent the twins to fetch fly-bags for them, that they did not breathe in a suffocating dosage of grasshopper.

Thus far, Beidermann is happy to tell us, thus far his own land has been spared—providentially so, says he—and tells us he watched from a mile's distance a plume like a flying serpent flow across the prairie and settle like smoke on his neighbors' fields, bypassing his own, toward which it at first seemed headed for certain. He does not ask what turned it, but makes his report as he busily twists a little bow into the cuff of each shirt sleeve, then tucks it tightly under itself to secure his sleeves against invasion: his pants he has already tied off with twine over the boot tops, his shirt's top button fastened tight, so the reddish flesh of his neck puckers over the sweaty collar.

The Widow is under siege, too, Beidermann announces; a sizeable tributary of the winged stream having descended upon her, allowing her clamorous geese to so stuff themselves, says Beidermann—the only one of us to summon a chuckle—that the gander has no honk left! He has been at the Widow's the afternoon before—gallant though unadmitted suitor that he is—to battle the scourge with her while her two little girls, not the most sensible children in Creation, huddled in the house in terror, for they saw the voracious hordes as a sign the world was ending and they were doomed to die under a pile of clicking insects. . . . Indeed, maybe not so silly—for who can foretell the final sign He will send up at the end?

But Beidermann has more important information: it was while burying the Widow Jenssen's vegetables to remove them from the invaders' predations, he tells us, that inspiration visited him. Now he points to its results: it is the awkward device he goes to unlimber from his wagon bed, brought along to me, he allows, that I may test its practical worth—and, doubtless, stand impressed by Beidermann's genius.

He seems inordinately proud—for the straight-forward Beidermann—of what he has fetched us. What it appears to be, as the twins rush to help him ease it off the wagon, is a large slab of sheet metal. It flops flat on the ground, sending grasshoppers spraying out from under it in all directions.

You see, lectures Beidermann, it will scoop them up and into the coal oil you put back here, where they will die. Can we hitch one of your teams to it? He spits out his chaw, and is ready.

I am doubtful of his proposal, but in any event my animals are far afield, except the black gelding with which Harris plows a hasty, crooked furrow around the tomatoes, the upstruck earth, I can see from the barn, more gray than black, so deep has the drouth penetrated; and into this shallow ditch Ma and August scoop what insects they can catch with their grain shovels—the insects leaping clear near as fast as they are shoveled in—and when there is a chance accumulation a few yards along, Harris lays over it a cover of straw which he sets afire, and joins his helpers in slapping at both errant flames and fleeing grasshoppers. Some few die.

I point out my horses a half-mile off—I am not prone to fetch them for dubious purposes; and Beidermann unhesitatingly unfastens his mammoth animals from the wagon—they seem too grand for his trivial intention—and hooks them to the chains bolted to the far ends of his invention; which, it takes no careful inspection to see, might well be a section of the metal wall pulled from off the Skiles' saloon or livery barn: an eight- or ten-foot length, three- foot deep, which, Beidermann explains, will slide smooth and flat across the ground while being drawn by the chains he has just hooked up: and in the back, a little trough having been hammered in and the back lip folded up, he now pours a gallon or two from the tin stored under his wagon seat, and this will drown the scooped-up insects. . . . His preparation complete, Beidermann takes command of the contraption by two handles nailed to the far ends of the metal that bear in toward the center, where he walks, grasping the handles and changing direction by muscular force, as with a walking cultivator.

Captain Beidermann orders, and his animals, having stood to their limit against the irritating insects, surge into their collars, sending asail the gouts stuck to their wet cheekpieces, and

Beidermann's invention slices like a sharply swung blade into the uneven ground of my yard, slicing off hummocks and bulges as neatly as any road scraper as it bucks its way into the garden.

Beidermann does a lively dance to keep the thing in hand: we must admire his agility, but that is all. This apparatus of his is no more than a piece of tin, a shiny trinket to distract a two-inch bug, and more suitable to a child and ponies than the looming Beidermann and his leviathan pair.

As if their hero is achieving something, the twins jump in delight, skipping behind, as Beidermann frantically hauls at reins and handles alike, one of each in each hand, and persuades his team past the cowhides with their crawling host, to the remnants of the potato vines, the last of their green stems no more than fibrous threads poking like nerve ends out of the boiling layer of grasshoppers, the potatoes themselves mostly out of reach underground, their stems too insubstantial for the gnawers to tunnel down through them as they do with the onions and radishes, to eat them from the inside out, leaving hollow balls in the earth. . . . Onto this quivering carpet goes Beidermann, his horses hawing in a prance, jawing their bits like circus ponies, while the twins attend the rig's progress, having stationed themselves at either end—perhaps Beidermann has so instructed them—and leap to free the device when an edge catches, as it does, on a clod or hummock, or digs cockeyed into the soft earth. Dust rises in a cloud to obscure the mass of grasshoppers also rising—or it may be that it is the other way around and the grasshoppers do the obscuring: it is all a blur.

From under the eaves of the barn, Cornelius and Henry look on, and at the far end of the garden I see Harris pull up the gelding, and I know without seeing it, the scorn on his face. He drops the handles of the walking plow, and with Ma and August, turns to watch Beidermann's animated advance. The metal pan bounces high as if kicked from beneath, and whipsaws wildly as the leading edge catches here and there, flicking tongues of coal oil with each jerk until the twins are splattered head to toe as they wrestle the seesawing ends with shouts of half delight and half alarm.

Beidermann, the sweating helmsman, yells at his team, at the twins, at the grasshoppers, at God in His Heaven, perhaps; and I wonder if he has lost command of more than just his contraption—which is moving too fast: earth springing up before and flying over behind: his horses cannot draw it slowly enough; no living horses could; and his prey in its abundance leaps with ease from out of his path, and three feet over find something else to chew.

Behind my shoulder, Otto says: Well, I see he got two hoppers there, but looks like a million going the other way.

Some few little beasts, to be sure, are sufficiently confounded by Beidermann's device to jump into it. When he has made one swath, Beidermann hauls up to wipe the sweat out of his eyes; he tips his machine sideways, and a few hundred oil-coated grasshoppers slide onto a bushel-sized greasy pile of dirt, vines, rocks, and other parts of Ma's garden: to this heap, Beidermann sets a match, and the twins dance around the sudden shiny flame, itself unseen in the bright sun, to stamp out wayward sparks; their oil-soaked trousers, shirts, and hair severely imperiled.

Earnest at his work, Beidermann pours another dose of coal oil into his machine, and swings it about to take a new swath. He seems set to do this as long as anyone will allow him.

He swings his horses around at the garden's end, and I walk to meet them, the mounds of insects flickering away from their hooves like splashed water; and I wave Beidermann to a halt. He is puffing, he wipes his face—this pursuit of ephemera is a heavy business. But I do not wish to insult his efforts. I point to the meager contents of his scraper.

It works a little, I say. But not enough.

Beidermann studies the poverty of his haul with a squinting eye, and I cannot tell by his look if he knows the measure of his foolishness. But he is not the Beidermann we know if he cannot tell me why it is a famous triumph.

Yaas, he slowly allows. Not so many hoppers, true, but I am scraping up the eggs these little bastards leave, and saving you from going through this again in another month.

If they can find anything left in a month, say I, they are welcome to it. Take a look. Does this look like there will be a single growing thing for a God damned bug to eat, let alone a man and his wife and boys?

This is more anger than I mean to show—but why should I hide it? Beidermann looks away, then curls the ends of his reins around his machine's handles.

Well, what I am trying to do here, he says, is give you a hand.

Sure enough, I say. And I will say that I appreciate your intentions. But when you go to experimenting with your machines, you might think to do it on your own place. I say this knowing he has escaped the scourge. There is no need to come here and play with me.

Here, here, says Beidermann, who is not likely to misperceive that the cause of my ire is as much his good fortune as my bad.

These bastards have not come down on me, at least not yet, as you well know. . . . This thing is an experiment. . . . I meant to help.

Am I to tell him how he can finally help? Am I to say he must feel the burden of misfortunes of his own for once; that he needs a few failures under his belt and then I will shake his hand? My own pettiness galls me; begrudging another's happy lot; but I am exasperated, too, more than that—overwhelmed by flood, fire, drouth, cattle gone down in storms, blight, a family more miserable than not, often; and now this devastation of insects. . . . And it chose to pass Beidermann by, so he comes with his toy to play with those laid to waste.

To be sure, say I. But you might think about confining your experiments to the Widow Jenssen and do not come here with any fool devices!

It surprises me a little, how hard these words come out; for I feel no push to reduce the proud Beidermann: he does not bring his machine to tease me, I know; he tells the truth there. But I am not Job, and when afflictions descend upon a man and he heaves to free himself, even a little, his lashing about may aggrieve others, as here Beidermann.

But if Beidermann is stung, he is not humbled. He slaps at the grasshoppers; his horses stomp, their harness rattling, and Beidermann comes around their tossing heads, close up to me, a blackness deep in his eyes, his coarse lips drawn down, and pokes the half-finger on his right hand to my breast: yet his voice is mild enough, as if the matter he addresses, for all its consequences to others, is not so filled with importance to a man of parts such as himself.

As I remember his words, they start like a sermon: For all the years you have lived, old man, he says, I guess you have still not learned what you should. For God-damned sure, you have not come across a fellow like myself, who if he is going to fool with you—if he is going to *play* with you—why, then everybody in the country is going to know it. Let me tell you: I figured this tin thing would do a job against these bugs—he bats them aside as he speaks—and if it did not turn out that way, well, I regret it, and you have my apology for it.

The twins crowd my elbows as he speaks, as if to urge me to take Beidermann's apology: these two know more of Beidermann than any of us. They eye him, me, Henry, Otto, Harris, uneasily: they know what in Beidermann is simple aggravation, irritation, anger, or killing rage; and what they see now, I cannot tell from their faces—and for a long time I have been uncertain whether they have come to weigh heavier on Beidermann's side than my own.

So you have mistaken me badly, says Beidermann. But I am not one to take it as too serious a matter, because a man has to keep in mind how hard you have been hit. All this time with no rain, and then these critters come down on you hardest of all.

I nod my full assent. But suddenly we have another voice, and it is Harris, the last of my boys I would choose to speak for me in any dispute.

Yes, that is true, Harris throws in loudly, having come up, shovel in hand, on Beidermann's other side, and while more than a match for him in scowls, he altogether lacks our neighbor's mild tone of reason. On his neck the strawberry mark is redder than usual—a bad sign.

He says: You bet the bastards have damn well hit us hardest of all, sure. But there is some they have not hit at all, and a suspicious man might want to know why that is, eh? A suspicious man and a dumb enough one, might be persuaded to ask himself a stupid question: What's this? Old *Bittermilk* did not shoo them over here, did he, eh? We can all have a good laugh at that dumb idea, can we not, eh?

Harris reaches out that big hand—they are all big-handed, these boys of mine, the grown ones, and now the twins that way too, big of body: the worst of it being that Harris, while biggest of any but Otto, is smallest in well-balanced judgment, even as he is biggest of all in temper; and far too big a complainer, too much a grumbler, a dour man, grown from a heavy-hearted boy; for all that when he ran bare-footed, Ma prodded him toward the cheerful ways of his brothers; her joking and stories the others prized, while he stared down and kicked at the dirt.... His big hand sweeps out and plucks up one of the mass of passing grasshoppers: this he holds pinched by its wings at arm's length toward Beidermann.

Recognize this feller, do ye? he says: he could be addressing the insect or the man.

With a flick of his hand Beidermann slaps the thing away: to him it is not the insult Harris intended, and he says: That little insect has more brains than you do.

It is this, I suspect, something rotten like this, that Harris hankers after, by way of proving up his sneering view of Beidermann, and also to fill his need to run a course counter to his brothers'. There is a black streak in him, as Ma has always said, laying it to a spooked element in her Klaus bloodlines; in that her grandfather, dead before she knew him, left a legacy of bloody wildness across the south of Indiana: the cause of it, as her relatives tell the story, pure inborn cussedness: a singular man with a singular appearance: three-inch strawberry mark on his cheek—not on his neck—upon which the whiskers he grew abundantly elsewhere would not take: mean to man and beast equally, it is said, he died murdered after long misuse of his wife and children and relatives of all description: knifed to death, he was; with praise and no reckoning for the murderer, his young son. . . .

But these are different times and a man must show some judgment in the way he lives his life among others; for he encounters too many in every aspect of living not to take into account their sensibilities; as Harris is not willing, or able, to do. . . . And perhaps a little of that lack is in Beidermann too, for all that he can better accommodate his inward self than can my reckless son; Beidermann, the sweating outward hulk of him, shoulders sloped; and grasshoppers flitting past with the sound of crystals in an ice storm.

We are all in this picture. The twins turn in agony, and Otto yells to Harris to put down the shovel; and Ma calls him back to finish his furrow as if he had simply tarried to get a drink: And my own school-marmish admonition, no more suitable to the circumstance:

You lay off this rough talk, you two. . . .

Beidermann looks at me down his grand nose, as though to say: Old man, it is late in the game to be teaching your son manners: while Harris, drawn by rage down his own blind path, hears not so much as a mouse's squeak of caution, as he steps up to raise his shovel.

He has more brains than me, does he, then? he says into Beidermann's face. Well, he God-damned well has more b---s than
you, you sorry excuse for a dog's p---k!

Ah! Beidermann must be given this: he does not appear to
have been called names by enough men for it to be commonplace, but he does not flinch or blink; although I cannot say the
same for myself; and Ma utters a throaty sigh; while Beidermann
stands cool as a man without fear or concern. . . . Indeed, he can
see there is call for neither—for Otto steps forward and in one
big motion wraps Harris around from behind, long arms clamp-
ing down like a vise; so there will be no swinging shovel, indeed,
no hostile move at all, no move of any sort; for, straining only
slightly, Otto removes his younger brother an inch off the ground
and swivels around so the two face away from Beidermann; Harris puffing and blustering the while over his shoulder as I step up
to loosen the shovel from his pinned hand. He is purple with
choler, and kicks back at his brother, who shows us a nimble
dance among the grasshoppers to keep his shins undamaged. But
Otto is much the stronger boy, and all Harris' inflamed exertion is
unavailing, for he is soundly snared. Indeed, there is enough in
him still sensible, so that he does not struggle to the degree that
Otto need hurt him, as he hops him like a frog some yards away,
close to the plow's handles, saying: I am going to tie you down to
this plow, if you do not stop this horses--t behavior!

Yaas! calls Beidermann. Hitch the bugger to it and let him
plow a few acres, to work some sense into him!

Harris, I would think, in his heightened state could almost do
it. But there is no fight now, nor promise of one, and no call for
taunts and jibes from either party. I step into Beidermann's way.

This is a sorry business, I say to him. I would never want to see it, and I know you are man enough to recognize it all as a mistake on my boy's part. It is not the way we do business with our neighbors, but this is a time when we are badly pushed, as you know.

Beidermann sizes me up. Yes, you can say that if you want to, old man, he says, calling me that again, which he has not done before today, this uncommon day, so his mockery is clear. But I am bound to see it my own way, and I will say this: your boy there knows where my fence lines are, and all he has to do is cross them one time, and I will show him the ways I do business with my neighbors when they do not show any more sense than he does.

He unhooks his team's traces from his device and backs the team to the singletrees of his wagon, hitches up, and heaves the tin sheet onto it—dirt and oil and the few grasshoppers still in it sail off in a ribbon, the greasiness of the mess catching a brief rainbow glimmer of sun.

We watch that, and we watch Beidermann. It is our tableau in the yard under the ugly noon sun: the grasshoppers form a landscape, and out of the dust of it arise their stridulations, a gibing chorus to the slap of our hands. The twins watch tormented as the pillar Beidermann is carried from them by their brother's foolish enmity; and as Beidermann yanks the fly-screens off his horses' heads, they look to Harris as if he may have it in him to offer a decent word and set things right; and they look to Ma as if she might smooth the rough business over with a piece of pie and cup of coffee; and they look to me . . . how? Perhaps as if I might haul myself up like Moses and deliver a pronouncement so wise, so profound, so all-embracing in the comfort it laves over all, that the sweaty lot of us will stagger into each other's arms, crying out

our folly. . . . and the twins will be off trapping weasels with Beidermann tomorrow. . . .

But what if I misread their look? And it is not hope that is in
it, but only censure? And better it be censure than hope, here, under the parching sun, amidst the awful insects, their hope, their
lack of it, their very hope of hope, matters not at all. What room
is there for a child's faith here? What expectation of joy reasonable in this heat, this blight?

I smolder, yes. Beidermann even at peace is not an easy man
to swallow, and we have him here rampant; and it cannot be, we
cannot have a wrathful neighbor, or else we look to another
war across the fence lines—and of those this country has seen
enough; lastly by the bellicose Krupp with his neighbor to the
north, Bruntz; their dispute over a ditch that one of them dug—
Krupp is the last man to make clear which—and thus distracted
the limb of Skunk Creek that crosses each property: and who was
right and who was wrong in that dispute remains unknown, although shots were fired in the night, fat-bellied Krupp told me
while maintaining himself an unlikely innocent victim; although
Bruntz, like the slop-bucket Dutchman he was, had not sense
enough to make his side heard, and in short time was busted and
gone—back to the wife's folks in Wisconsin, no doubt; and from
the poor look of his place he was headed there soon enough with
or without Krupp's vagrant ditches and skulking midnight pot-
shots. . . .

Otto takes his hold off Harris' shoulder but stands beside him
close as a prison guard, and Beidermann sets one foot on a horizontal spoke of his wagon wheel and swings himself up to the
bench. As one, the twins come up, as if they might wave him off

down the lane and run behind in the dust for a little way, as they sometimes do. They wait, their faces desolate.

Stepping up, I lay one hand on the big rump of Beidermann's mare, slapping grasshoppers off it, and take a bead up the reins to Beidermann's face; but before I can offer any moderate word, Beidermann speaks: If you like the feel of my horse's ass, old man, he says, maybe you would like mine, too. Well, I can make it available for kissing by that red-faced boy of yours.

For that one moment I am willing to give up on the insolent Beidermann: there are several of us here who in two minutes can render the smart fellow, for all his size and muscle, such a lesson for his sass as he will record in his memoirs. Should I be ashamed to say it? I could have set the boys on him like dogs, the twins alone holding back. . . . And then we are all barbarians again. . . . If I am a Christian man, as I am, then I know where I stand here: no case for turning the other cheek is ever better made, a school book example, quite as if the Almighty Himself has hand-fashioned it expressly as a test—should the drouth and grasshoppers be insufficient—by way of showing His floundering servant how fragile is the stitching of one's faith, how near the surface, weakness. . . .

Beidermann, Beidermann, I call to him, haughty on his wagon seat, this is no good. I can see I am too hasty in my criticism of you. I know your intention is neighborly . . . But it is these damned bugs: they will kill everything alive, and friendship and neighborliness are included in the victims, and I cannot abide to see us taken in by the effect of them. Beidermann, we have all had a bad season—. But there I stop, for Beidermann has not had a bad season.

Now he hoists the reins above the swinging tails of his team and measures me with a coal-black eye.

Bugs are bugs, he says. The bugs will go, but I will still be here. It was not bugs that give me hard words. It was your boy there——. He pokes his bristled chin at Harris, who growls as if he is a damn dog. Our neighbor slaps the reins lightly on the horses' backs, dislodging a few dozen grasshoppers, and the team steps out.

Harris bawls some last word—I am so disgusted with him I cannot listen—and Otto, much provoked, shoves him back; and Beidermann's rig departs down the ruts of our road in an eddy of dust and grasshoppers, his contraption rattling loudly in the wagon bed. The twins try to look at me but cannot; and Ma shakes her head back and forth, pursing her lips and looking at me and shaking her head. . . .

Presently Otto retrieves the shovel, hands it to the boiling Harris, and turns away, saying: That son of a bitch might at least take his bugs with him. . . .

Now, WITH TIME TO RECRUIT ourselves somewhat, well may we ask: When will we see our stalwart neighbor again? We have our grasshoppers still, but we do not have our Beidermann; and if we measure their ruinous stay against his bitter departure, which are we to lament the more?

AUG. 20. A sop chucked down to us: they go at last. At milking time, when I walk to the barn, it is without the dismal crunch underfoot. One by one, two by two, they have picked up and sailed away. Obeying what magical signal? What signal needed beyond the ravished landscape they have left? Holes in the dirt where onions grew; fork handles filigreed; barren box elders and cottonwoods; a half-dozen hens dead of gluttony and the eggs of the survivors too bug-laced for the taste of any but the stuffed and snorting hogs; a little of the garden is saved, under the hides: Ma's geraniums wilted but living, under the holey quilts.

Look, says Henry, waving his hand. You can see for a half-mile before there is anything alive.

AUG. 21. But some hang back, so attached are they to our largesse: in the house, a few still. . . . One straggler now creeps toward my lamp—to fatten on the oil, perhaps, to consume the very flame, to bring us news of the unregenerate Beidermann; this specimen no less brash than our neighbor, choosing to rest saucily before my lamp, a hand's breadth from my pen, unaware of the hatred mantling in me. By my page the creature stands unmoving, then quivers, coarsely adjusts his stiff and gauzy wings, and tucks in his drumstick legs as if readying them for use. For all his diminutive size he is not dainty, but crude, his aspect rank, his single adornment the pearls of light caught on the sawteeth on the backs of his legs. His buffalo head is all eye and jowl: he faces me straight on, undaunted by my moving pen, although his feelers poke up alert, twitching one way or another, eyes fixed. He does not see what I am, but senses it. If I turn my hand quickly to the side it will crush him—for the feeble plate of armor across his back protects him in his world, but not in mine. Or is that my mistake, and it is indeed his world?

SOMETHING LIKE THE LITTLE fizz that Fourth of July root beer, cold as ice, would send up his nose, now buzzed through his whole damn head. It happened before and he didn't always know why, but this time he did know.

He sat cross-legged, just barely hidden in the tall grass, north of Beidermann's place. His sack and rifle—not *his* rifle exactly, but shared in use and upkeep with August and Henry, although they didn't know he had taken it—lay in his lap, and he watched the big-mouth son of a bitch down there wait with pin in hand for the moment to set it into the windmill's drawbar; a little slip and he could lose a joint or two or a fingernail, but no such luck; and for all the brisk breeze, the windmill slowed as it took up its pumping labor. Dust rising high, the cattle crowded to the trough.

All heifers, not a bad-looking herd even from this distance. The late sun angled down so as to put them partly in shadow, but he could tell they were yearlings, twenty or more, nearly as many as Pa had. That was a surprise.

The view Harris so carefully took of Beidermann and his live-stock was from a growth of blue-stem on a gentle bluff a quarter-mile off. He considered himself not so much hidden as only obscured: looking hard and long enough, Beidermann could spot him if he wanted to. He gave the son of a bitch that chance.

Behind him, past the break of the bluff, stood the only damn thing he knew he owned for sure. Nobody else wanted it, a twenty-year-old gelding, nameless, called when necessary "Harris' nag" or "the old bay," waiting with hanging head, reins tucked needlessly under a rock: it was used to these hidden waits.

From his grassy seat Harris, with one eye on the hounds that lingered at the windmill with their boss, overlooked the pigpen, noting it was a safe distance from the doomed barn. No reason for the hogs to be harmed; among the animals he dealt with, hogs were not so bad, considering the slobbering, manure-laden cattle; and stubborn horses that would ruck you against a stall-side, or stomp on your foot, or bite you in the back with green-stained teeth the size of dominoes when you bent over to pick up a wagon tongue; and brainless chickens that would go any direction but the one you shooed them to.

In a snuff tin in his shirt pocket he had the dope, and in the sack the chopped-up chunks of mud-cats from the creek, their ugly heads with the poisonous barbs hacked off, wrapped in two thicknesses of oil skin filched from a pile of bits and pieces of just about anything that Ma had been saving for as long as he could remember. Even double-wrapped, they smelled like sin, be-ing two days old—that was the one thing that made him anxious, that smell. He knew the wind here, but still he kept testing to make sure it was still coming at him. It would be trouble if the hounds caught the scent before he meant them to.

What he waited for was a little less light, and for Beidermann to go into his house or barn and the hounds to be out of sight. It might take a while, but he knew how to wait for what he wanted—or to simply wait for whatever happened. More than once he had scrunched himself in tall grass just about everywhere hereabouts, and he had seen himself some things, sure enough: Blauser with a halter rope, whaling at his old woman by the barn door while their half-dozen kids bawled and tried to hide behind the outhouse; the Faust boy throwing rocks at the shypoke in his old man's swamp, stringing out his dinger and trying to wrestle his dog into licking it; one of the Krupp boys, trolling along well north of the family property, snicking off one of Rylander's straggling bull calves, neat as you please, and hazing it back onto his old man's land; and big Clarence Schneider scooting like an over-grown shit house rat across the Widow Jenssen's yard in early evening, to duck out of sight into a ravine by the river where a horse might well be tied, and if he wasn't pulling up his britches as he ran he might as well have been; and then soon enough, her hair down, the Widow strolls out to collect the eggs.

And always more . . . old lady Blauser tip-toeing into the creek's reedy washes to give herself a good bath with a chunk of lye soap the size of a brick, not letting it touch the red welts across her shoulders. . . .

Just so did he watch Beidermann as he came and went, with pails, with a fork, with a basket of corn, in the fading light. Mostly, the hounds lay quietly in the dust, and when their boss came near raised their heads to see if anything of interest offered itself. Now Beidermann strode purposefully from the barn to the corncrib and knelt to look under. For this, the hounds hurried along. What was he looking for? Rats? The hounds didn't think so; they sniffed the boss's upraised rear end and strolled away. Maybe some old biddy had laid a clutch under there. That tickled Harris—Beidermann coddling his setting hens. . . . But then he thought, Well, wouldn't that be a good place to stash a jug? Even though Beidermann was hardly required to hide his hooch—unless, maybe, the Widow had got to him with her talk. And in fact, he remembered that winter when Beidermann was laid up at the Widow's, and they had gone through his place, his jug out in the open on the shelf by the fancy plates. . . . Harris had got himself a good taste of it too, until Pa put his foot down.

About enough light was left for him to put together his baits. He took out the oilskin packet and unfolded it with some care. The day's heat had worked on the fish, and he was reluctant to put that much smell into the open air, but if he worked quickly, and the wind didn't get tricky. . . .

With a stick he poked holes in the yielding flesh, working it around to enlarge the base within, and into these he forced as much of the dope from the snoose can as would fit. He made sure to use it all, spilling some, but he had plenty, not knowing how reliable it was, although old Schneider, in whose machine shed he had snooped out an open sack of it, claimed he had put down more coyotes with it than anyone around, and a couple of wolves too, although no one had seen the wolves.

When he had six soft nuggets, each the size of a baby's fist, he gave up, throwing the rest of the rotting fish as far away as he could, way past the ragged bay, who didn't like the smell any more than he did.

Around him the grass had collected the beginning of the evening dew, and Harris wiped his hands in this, not much diminishing the smell; but now he had his baits at hand. And he had the sling, from out of the spider webs in the barn—at least he thought it was his, he'd had one like it once, and damn well knew how to use it too. He'd knocked down a good number of squirrels years ago and proudly tacked their tails to the barn door, but rats or the cats always eventually made off with them.

It was nearly dark now. He could still see the shapes of the hounds, and to someone who didn't know dogs, they might look asleep. It was simple enough, Harris saw: if he moved ten or twelve rods to the west, the barn would be between him and the dogs. He'd sling those baits to the barn's offside so that where they came from was hidden, and the baits themselves unseen. . . . Unseen but, by God, *smelled!* And once the hounds had gobbled down their goodies, well, then Beidermann would get a treat of his own.

There was a crack or two in the canvas of the sling, but nothing serious. This would work fine. With each swing, he flung out two pieces of fish. *Whoop, whoop!* His horse stirred at the sound, or maybe the smell.

In the dark he couldn't be certain, but the baits looked to have gone where he'd intended. He wiped his hands again, the grass wetter now.

He waited. The smell surely had blossomed fully across the yard. Even now, as they dozed, the dogs' noses would be furiously atwitch.

He sat quietly, hearing nothing, as the night chill descended.

. . .

A STAR POPPED OUT. He saw it. It wasn't there and then it was; then more and it was dark around him.

Only silence from below, no movement, nothing to be seen. The lamp that had burned for a half-hour in Beidermann's window was long out. Surely he was asleep . . . though not so deeply as his dogs.

Harris stood, carefully stretching his cramped legs, and turned his head to catch a sound—a faint convulsive coughing whine, from past the barn and barely heard. Nothing to fear. Through the wet grass, he walked to his stoic gelding and retrieved the lard can hung by its bale from the pommel. This smelled too, but he would take the smell of kerosene over rotten fish any day.

In many ways this night was no different from any other; the wind died considerably but would be back tomorrow, the dew so heavy he felt it against his face, and the silence of the grave all around.

With half an eye on the house he moved around to the northeast corner of the barn, hurrying—with the kerosene sloshing out as he ran—and heard a heavy, thick sound within the straw-chinked wall. All them cats, he thought; no, a big animal. Too late now. He was at the corner of the barn with his match ready and, scratching it across his pant leg, touched it delicately down.

And there she goes, he thought, looking back. No big, sky-high conflagration—he didn't want that—but just those little flicks all along the bottom of the barn, like a rough and brightly drawn line. There was nowhere for it to go but up . . . and then out, and across, and turn a corner, and around and about and up higher still, and then the tarpaper on the roof. . . . There she goes. . . .

Harris, his bay gelding moving at a nice trot, didn't look back again.

CLOSE TO MIDNIGHT; he had never been in town this late. Only a couple of lights shone, one small yellow one in Schwantz's window. Harris tangled his horse's reins in the sunflower stalks that grew in the lot south of the Mercantile—an even weedier lot was to the north of the narrow building. Fingering the coins in his pocket, he opened the crooked screen door, considering what sort of traveling eats he would need. Some crackers, some beans, a can of peaches if he had the money.

A small lamp with an untrimmed wick that sent up strings of black smoke cast a meager light on Schwantz and the man he was talking to at the table he used for a counter. Harris didn't know the customer and couldn't quite tell in the near-darkness, but he might have been redheaded. He had a stoop-shouldered slouch to him.

Schwantz said, "Howdy, my boy." Harris figured he didn't know his name, but he knew the family. "How's your daddy getting on? Don't believe I seen him since the Fourth."

He hated this sort of exchange; it was always happening. He mumbled something and walked past the possible redhead to a barrel holding a jumble of packaged hard crackers.

The stranger pulled his head back as Harris passed, and gave a low whistle. "Wowee, you got some powerful perfume there, my friend. You been rolling with your dogs in rotten fish, or what?"

He chuckled, looking to Schwantz, who only wiped his hands on his apron.

Harris made no reply; he laid out three dimes on the table for the crackers and beans, and then another nickel for the sack of tobacco he pointed to Schwantz to give him. The storekeeper took the coins and slipped them somewhere under the table. "Gettin' colder," he said.

Harris nodded. Schwantz and his store had been there from the first he could remember; he had heard that his wife had died long ago and a couple of children had fled forever to Saint Paul and Chicago. Harris didn't mind that the old man had more than once called him "Otto."

Purchases in hand, Harris turned to go; the redhead had closed in as if to get a closer whiff of the fishy perfume—or to get a look at the wine-stain mark on Harris' neck. He was a lumbering fellow, bent over at his big shoulders as if to pay close attention to small men, and he had a smell of his own, from the saloon. He peered down at Harris, wrinkling his nose, saying, "Now, that is some stink my friend. I ain't smelt nothin' like that since that old whore in Zimmerman ast me to check her crotch to see what that rash was."

Schwantz turned and walked to the back of his store, where he was only a shadow in the small light. Harris fixed the redhead with a stare and, with the big man smirking after him, walked without haste through the misaligned screen door: it had been askew like this since he was a small boy and been handed once a year, perhaps, a penny candy from a much happier Schwantz.

Amidst the sunflower stalks, his ragged bay waited as patiently as ever. Beside it, Harris stood for a time, looking into the dark, stroking his animal's nose and remembering the old man's mealy-mouthed advice for solving youthful indecision: *In for a penny, in for a pound.* Then he slipped his rifle free of its strap on the saddle, stepped quickly to the front of the Mercantile, and without aiming fired one shot from his hip through the screen door; then, more quickly yet, he pushed back through the sunflower stalks to his animal and rode briskly south, the night becoming starrier and brighter as he went.

He wasn't sure he was awake. In his window it was bright and dark all at once, a jumble of shadow and lightning. But no thunder. Perhaps the sound of a strong breeze.

He jammed his legs into trousers, pulling on a coat as he ran out, drew up short, the warmth hitting him; his barn wholly packaged in flame; and there was no thinking any one thing first—all that hay gone—what was in there? The mare he had swapped for—all that hay. Jesus Christ! All that hay!

It was far gone already. He saw that at once. Too far gone for anything to be done. The water trough was hardly three rods from the flames but might as well have been a mile for all the good a puny few buckets of water could do now. He didn't have a chance to do a Goddamned thing, the barn half gone before he knew it was afire. The dogs? Not a peep from them—and they should have torn the bastard apart.

And now he saw why they had not; running to the west side of the flames, he stumbled, almost fell, over what was left of the bitch. On his knees he took up her head and in the wild light saw her jaw agape, lips drawn back, tongue aflop. He had seen many a coyote carcass looking just the same after a good dose of strychnine. . . . Schneider's strychnine, always, Schneider being the only one hereabouts who fancied that particular dope—but surely it wasn't Schneider—and why would she ever take it? He thought of the pups she carried—some of them promised and traded for— and smelled fish on her face.

And nothing he could do. Heated by the flames, he ran back to the porch, grabbed his rifle, and fired three shots into the air, knowing as he did so that this alarm might have effect in daylight prairie blazes, but now the few people who might hear it were asleep. . . . His thoughts were all ascatter. God Almighty, all that hay, and that lame mare, tied in there to get her off her bad leg for a time. No animal movement in the flicker-lit yard, the yearlings and his big Percherons and the milkers having rushed to the far limits of their pasture; he hoped not beyond, panicked into tearing through the feeble excuse for a fence he had strung up back there.

With the useless rifle in one hand, he ran round to the east of the barn. The burning alfalfa sent wafts of scent almost like the crushed herbs the Widow sometimes brewed into a suffusion she claimed was healthy. . . . All that good alfalfa . . .

And there lay the black hound; and the smartest dog he had ever had smelled of fish too. It was beyond belief.

His losses racked themselves up in his head. All that alfalfa, and timothy and swamp hay, that was all gone, his dogs poisoned, and the pups done in, the four he had promised to Johansen for the ragged little team of sorrels; and now the mare, in the barn, gone, burned up, God Almighty; her partner way off with the rest of the cattle, he hoped; but if not—

Behind him, roused by the flames, a rooster crowed, and in the hen house, cackling started up. He should have had geese, like the Widow, or guinea hens, full of warnings day or night.

Before the fiery stump of his barn, a high spurt of flame darted out suddenly and then died down to a glow, the whole furious mass of it higher than Beidermann's head, but crumbling here and there to waist level, with a shower of sparks.

Sparks; he remembered the gusts of sparks when his old man's barn had burned—less a barn than a shed, a lean-to, really, barely sheltering the pair of cross-eyed, ugly-tempered black mules through the grim winters just short of the Canadian line. How that meager structure had ever caught fire and burned as fiercely as it did was a mystery to Beidermann, who at age twelve had watched in awe and delight as it went up. Well, he knew more than one affronted neighbor had reason to want prickly old Adolf Beidermann's holdings to suffer, Leo himself entertaining occasions when he longed for the old man to kick the bucket, most determinedly when his pa had nixed the free pup old Vogelsang wanted to give Leo, claiming his damn kid was too lazy to take care of it, when all along it was Leo who fed and wormed and brushed the gaunt pair of killers the old man called his own but never took out unless some crony came around with a jug, wanting some company for a drunken chase. He was a little over fourteen when he got himself up and went south, and with two years gone since the lean-to burned, the author of the deed never uncovered, for all the old man's armed forages and ranting accusations, the mules now huddled beside the tiny haystack, tails to the winter wind.

Some green timber in his barn had life left, and popped like rifle fire; burning bits tipped down into the huge mound of burned-over hay, which looked like nothing so much as glowing dust. . . . *That* was his hay. And in December, when his animals breasted the drifted snows in the yard to reach the hay he threw down, then what would he throw to them? A small glimmer of possibility—the heavy growth surrounding the swamp, sawgrass to make a heifer's mouth bleed, but some nourishment in it. With a scythe he might get a couple of loads—but he needed fifty, or more.

Behind him the young sow and her pigs, the progeny of Praeger's big red boar, stirred uneasily in the flickering light, the sow grunting with such primeval heaviness that the sound seemed to come from underground, and kept her family calm.

He looked east, calculating the time. The glow from the barn having faded, the washed bluish-milk hue of the dawn showed over the even lay of the land, an autumnal sky promising a cold day and morning dew to settle the last embers of his hay. The last, he thought, the last. . . .

Before it got so light that he could not avoid facing the crueler details of his job, he got the spade from where it rested against the hayrack, its handle still warm, and halfway between the granary and his outhouse, where the chickens had located their favorite dust bath and the soil was soft, he dug a grave for his two dogs, and laying them in side by side, he filled in the hole with care, saving the driest, softest earth for last, so the chickens would still have their place.

Catastrophe
for Beidermann,
and Others

⚜

⟶ 1887 ⟵

OCT. 30. In this ledger I have recorded more than once, as they occur, both salubrious days and insalubrious ones, and surely there is little in the date set down above to qualify it as one of the former; and no one in my family so unfortunate as to witness the calamitous early forenoon visit of our neighbor—once our *good* neighbor, although few here now would assign him that benign standing; surely no one with the surname of Praeger—who will not say that this common observation shines with the clarity of a solemn and dreadful truth, indeed.

And yet, however manifest that truth, it presents difficulty for me to set down on this page what turmoil and suspenseful anxiety our day has been thrown into—and the Good Lord only knows how many days and nights to come, likewise—by our visit from the fractious Mister Beidermann, with his bold impeachment of the Praeger name.

Even as I sit here, these hours later, thinking a clear and straight thought is not easy. For who among us has heard such foul charges from the mouth of a once civil man; indeed one, who by his own bedstead keeps a copy of the Christian Bible: I have seen it there. And yet this man, a man of some probity I once thought, whom we called neighbor, even friend, now heaps upon us like piles of manure, imprecations and accusations we can scarcely comprehend; he foams like a mad dog. But in all the roar of his fury and gesticulation atop his unfamiliar sorrel colt upon which he rides up, there is no doubt who has roused his agitation to such a level: it is Harris. Harris has undone him; but it is a while before the meaning of his charges unfolds, as he catches his thoughts together, in a way less excited individuals can comprehend.

Before then, as he comes through dust up the road, Otto spots him soon enough, saying: There is a colt we have not seen before. We will learn its history, as the twins race up to grab its bridle, one of them saying: This is Johansen's pony, one of them!

Beidermann swings off the saddle, and utters the last civil words we shall hear from his mouth, as he tells the twins: Yes, I got the pair of them off Bud. You lads should of been there: we made some swap: that ragged pair of ponies for four pups off that litter from my bitch.

Beidermann looks down at them, their eyes glittering, and he says: Eight, ten days, they are due. Bud gets the pick. . . . That is, he would of . . . And he grows ominously silent, glaring at us all.

The twins draw surprised faces: those high-bred hounds with their Canadian pedigree he values so dear—it seems like the unimpressive colt and his mate are no prizes, no doubt, but they say nothing.

Cornelius, however, does speak out, laughing: Four little pups for a team? And who agreed to that deal, sober?

I would think that by now Cornelius, and all my boys, would have learned better than to scoff at Beidermann; but no. And across the nose of his sweaty, shabby recent acquisition, Beidermann leans into Cornelius' face, saying: Which one are you? August? Naw, August has some sense. So you think Bud got cheated, eh? I got him drunk and f--ked him out of his horses, eh?

Now he is straight into Cornelius' face, spitting into the boy's eye with the violence of his speech: One of those pups, sir, is worth any f--king horse you ever rode, sir! And *two* of those pups, *dead*, are worth any one of you, you Praegers!

Otto raises an unavailing hand, bemused.

Beidermann swings his arms to take in everyone in the whole section, yelling: And my hay! What is that worth? I tell you what it is worth—it is worth every c-k-r in this whole f--king Praeger clan! Every f--king one, I tell you!

We stand aghast, to a man, audience to such filth, and why: Beidermann has his quirks, yes, but what is this?

And, he answers that question, at last, in his own perverse way: Where is Harris? he cries. Where is he? that mis-marked bastard son of yours?

He is spouting spittle and foam, like some virulent dog guarding the River Styx, barking and snarling.

Where is he? I mean to have a word with him, old man. Where is that s--t-pants Praeger who poisons my dogs and burns my barn? Where is he?

We can only stand astonished; that from out of his vile onslaught comes such a fairy-tale accusation: in this fulsome rant, an especially execrable nugget! And he connects Harris to this? This crime he shouts out at us?

From the porch, having heard a little of Beidermann's offensive discourse—surely not all or she would have fled into the house, hands over her ears—Ma comes halfway down the steps, speaking up: You ask after Harris, then? Well, he is not here, and he has not been here since first thing yesterday. So you are wasting your time with your loud talk, Leo.

I think not, says Beidermann. I have some regard for your brain, Missus, for although you married a Praeger you are saved from being born one; but you may not know the ugly workings of your boy's mind as well as I do—and surely not as well as my dogs do, poisoned by his hand; or the lame mate to this colt here, cooked up like a damn chunk of mutton by that coward with his matches and kerosene—you can still smell it. Come on over and get yourselves a sniff. You can smell the rotten fish he used on my dogs too. Come on, old man, hitch up that fancy buggy and come take a look at a masterpiece the Praeger family has produced; bring the missus, bring the whole damn tribe!

Otto cries out: Beidermann, you get yourself off this land now! You come here accusing—

Beidermann is louder still: I am not *accusing*, my fat friend, I am stating the truth. My dogs are dead of poison, my barn is burned, nothing left of it stands higher than that pus-gut of yours. And so

I have no hay for the winter—ah, perhaps I can keep alive on one milker with what I can scrape up. He waited until I had it all in, to make a better fire, eh? Now, let me ask you this, since I cannot ask your fine brother Harris: Will you haul a few dozen loads of hay over to my place before it snows? Are you going to furnish enough fodder to get a hundred and twenty head through until spring? What are they going to eat, eh? Out on the range? One good storm and they cannot get through the snow to whatever old grass is underneath. My horses might, but not them cows. A couple of storms and half of them will be froze to the ground like marble statues. . . . Hah, but what I might do—yes, I think I will—is drive every damn one of them over here, right here in your yard, and then if you do not fancy feeding them, let them freeze their damn muzzles to your porch step instead of mine; and the Praeger family can get out their shovels and bury the stinking mess, eh? Hey? And I will bet a dollar you can make some good money even out of that, eh, old man? Skin them all and sell their hides and bones for a nice price—hell, you will probably sell some of it back to me—and raise enough money to buy me out, eh? If I am still alive then, living off the flesh of my butchered horses.

But how are we, how is anyone, to bear such pained discourse? Beidermann, I say to him: Beidermann, here, here—

The twins are nearly in tears, and turn their faces aside, as they still hold the colt's bridle: they know well Beidermann's hounds; and when he built his barn they helped him shave the poles for it, and more.

Ma has come closer, her ears still uncovered, and says: We are very sorry for what you tell us. It is a terrible thing. But Harris is not here: I can tell you only that . . . and that no boy of ours was raised to . . . poison dogs . . . or burn down a man's barn—

Out of Beidermann's throat comes a coarse explosion, perhaps a laugh. Yaas, Missus, he says: And when I ride out of here I am going to visit all the mothers who did raise their boys to poison dogs and burn down barns—.

I hold up my hand: Mr. Beidermann, sir, you have had a history of disputes with Harris; it has been rocky between you, I know; and now this misfortune of yours—

Misfortune! bellows Beidermann like a madman. You think I stubbed my toe? For Christ's sake, my barn is *gone,* my dogs are dead—not just dead, poisoned, old man, by one of your kin—.

Ma has untied her apron and waves it now like a flag of truce. Leo, she says: this is a terrible thing you have suffered, terrible. Yes, we will help you, surely. But Harris is not here, and has not been for two days.

She looks at me, and at the ground, and quietly says: I want to know where he is too.

Well, says Beidermann, that makes three of us: you, me and Pfeiffer. But his tone has moderated somewhat; he is running out of his steam of fury; as indeed, no man could sustain it for long, and his heart not burst.

He turns back to his horse, takes the reins from the twins, and with a cruel grimace, says: I have a neighborly invitation for you all: come visit and see the remains of my barn, and where my dogs are buried. Without waiting for a reply, he hoists himself into the saddle.

Leo! calls Ma, fluttering her apron as he turns the colt. Would you take a chicken with you, then? The boys can dress it in a minute.

But for the twins I am closest to Beidermann, and I see across his face a panoply of expression, and perhaps a strangled smile, as his colt dances sideways.

No, ma'am, says he: it was not my chickens that burned.

And then he goes. . . . And leaves us all in a bog of dread wonder and suspicions beyond number and the feel of ruin. . . .

I have not heart enough to write more tonight. . . . And where is Harris?

NOV. 1. If we are to receive a caller this frosty morning, and it is other than Emil Pfeiffer, then someone has tinkered with the way matters work hereabouts, in circumstances where accusations may be flung about, regardless.

He comes up, his furry mittens holding the reins to as neat a pair of gray fillies as a man would hope to see, pulling his triple-shellacked buggy; the whole of it is more than any of us without a government salary can honestly aspire to; all full of how-de-do as he draws this handsome equipage to a stop amongst our uneasy dogs at the porch steps.

Going out, I reach for a thick coat. Well, Emil, say I, this is an early visit.

Yes, yes, yes, it is, he calls out, staying put on his slick-varnished bench. Cold as a witch's tit, aint it?

He wears some sort of wolf-furred collared overcoat, its hide seeming a half-inch thick. By God! I like to froze. And it aint even snowed yet, either.

True, true, say I. The steam of our breath, and the huffs of his team send up vaporous clouds all around. In the road the mud is frozen into twisted ruts, providing our visitor with a most roly-poly approach, for all his well-sprung vehicle; but nothing subtracts from his lawman-like demeanor, which perhaps he has learned from magazine pictures—formal, upright, stern of visage—yet, by nature, puny and stoop-shouldered; and if he sees himself as a hero of justice, there are more than a few who see him as a horse's ass.

For all the chill, Ma, who has been whipping eggs at the stove, comes out in her shirt; whether to have some word on the desperate matter that has kept her without sleep, or to invite our chilled visitor in for breakfast, I cannot say. Cornelius comes forth too, twisting suspenders over the shoulders of his underwear sleeves, and to Otto, just behind him, he says: I be damned if that Beidermann aint swore a warrant out on us, on Harris. Otto gives him a shove, saying, Shut your mouth.

If he has thoughts of descending from his perch to join us amongst the circling dogs by the porch, Emil abandons them, stuck to his polished seat; and says: So how you been, Gerhardt? Aint seen you since the Fourth, I do believe. He nods to Cornelius and Otto: Boys, he says; and at the same time touches his heavy wool cap and calls over their heads to Ma: Missus, you looking okay this morning.

From all this he receives no response, but he maintains a pleasant look. To me, he says, Yes, indeedy, some cold weather a-coming. I seen sundogs, and look at my team here, the way that hair is growing in.

Yes, Emil, say I: It is winter and I do not dispute it.

As if I have uttered words of wisdom he nods, and from his fine perch leans down toward me, saying in a confidential way:

Gerhardt, I rode over here to see if I could talk with your boy, Harris. Do you suppose he is anywhere handy where I could see him for a minute?

He smiles, or smirks, as a sign of bogus friendliness; but it is only plain aggravation to Cornelius, who calls out: What the hell business do you have talking to him for?

Our proper lawman raises his eyebrows at this, but looks not to Cornelius but to me, and I raise a hand to shut the boy off, for all that I agree with his feeling. But for Ma, among them all he is the gloomiest, grim and unspeaking, in that he is closest to Harris in age, the two separated by less than a full year: they had a way of looking out for each other, playing as youngsters in the swamp, or running through the winter storms to school together, their dinner in the same pail.

To me, Pfeiffer says: I was hoping to have a talk with Harris. Might be, we could straighten some things out easy enough. You know, It aint like me to be hard with my neighbors.

Emil, say I, I would help you out here, if I could. The fact is, Harris is not here. I do not know where he is; there is nobody here who knows, for he has been traveling the last few days. He has a way of doing that, going off. . . . And, saying this, I am thinking: God will forgive me, surely, as this is my son. . . .

And when he turns up here again, well, we will find out where he has been and see what he has to say for himself; that is, about what you want to talk to him about. . . . Boys, they go off. You can understand how that is, being the father of boys yourself.

Pfeiffer stares down at me, without a word, as if a response will only humiliate us both; but Otto steps up: Listen, if you got questions for Harris, go ahead, shoot, we will answer them.

Pfeiffer shakes his head, but tolerantly. Otto is not done; he is never quite done: Listen, if it is Beidermann who sent you here, you are on a fool's errand; and let me ask you this: Where is your damn warrant?

Pfeiffer blows out a steamy breath. I have been mistook here, boys, says he. Nobody is talking about a warrant, then. But, Hell's fire, I am a sworn officer and I have got to follow what the law says; and when there is anything to do with a shooting, that is to say, the unlawful discharge of a weapon in such a manner as to endanger the public safety, then certain duties do fall to me.

From behind me, murmurs: *Shooting? Shooting?* And I might well add my own whispering question to them. I say: Emil, there is no soul standing here, or anywhere on my land, who can tell you anything about a shooting.

I do not doubt your word, Gerhardt, and I will agree that what you say is so—nobody *here.* But we have Schwantz himself who tells me this. You know him as well as I do—better, I would say. How long you been trading with him, you and the missus? A lot of years, eh? Back when his kids were still around helping him, I bet. Well, Schwantz, I do not see him lying about this, and besides, there was a witness, this big overgrown redhead name of Kirchoff, works for that hide-shipper Foss, comes through every once in a while, got that yard south of town where they used to have the mule pens. Maybe you know him, great big fuzzy-headed boy, got one eye wanders to the south a lot? His old man went bust near Friedrich five, six years ago and hauls everybody back East, except this big kid would not go. I guess he figured he could make a dollar here as easy as he could a dollar there. He sure as hell aint the kind of boy who could make much more than that, no matter if he is in Minnesota or Wisconsin or anyplace else. . . . He would rattle on until dinner. I call out: What is this *shooting*, then? You claim there was a shooting—.

Gerhardt, he says, what I *claim* has nothing to do with the matter; we are talking about the discharge of a firearm in a public habitation witnessed by two people. It is a fact, not a claim, for I have seen the hole in Schwantz's screen door and in the back, in a beam over that big pickle barrel of his, a big splintered hole where the slug is. You can come and take a look at it yourself.

Emil, say I: I have to say I am tired of getting invitations to inspect ravages hereabouts. I already have one from Beidermann.

Of course, says Pfeiffer, of course, Beidermann would do that. I know the talk about Leo's barn going up, and his poisoned hounds—damn, I sure do hate to hear about poisoned dogs. I tell you, Gerhardt, I bet most men would rather be known to shoot a man than to poison a dog . . . well, maybe not if the man died. . . . Those were real high-bred hounds he had, too; some pups on the way worth a bunch, too. . . .

Out of patience once more, Otto says: Sheriff, you go on and on about shooters and poisoners and barn burners, and you do not have a warrant and there is none of the whole crew here, whom you keep talking about.

Ah, says Pfeiffer in a wily way: I think you have hit on it, Otto, not *here,* but then where? Where is Harris?

Now I have no more patience than Otto: Wait, wait just a minute, Emil. I am still not sure what you claim; but how, in any reasonable way, do you fasten this to my boy?

Gerhardt, you see, the law works this way: let me explain it to you all plainly. I have Schwantz and this big redhead testifying to the illegal occurrence, as follows: the two of them are in the Mercantile, late, having a chat, although I have never known Schwantz to be much of a talker. Harris comes in—now, Schwantz was not sure of the first name—he knew it was not Otto—but he swore it was a Praeger, the one with the wine-colored cheek, and he buys himself four bits' worth of stuff—Schwantz says, beans, crackers, like that; and this big redhead is talking to him—Schwantz says he did not know what was said, until he realized the big kid told the Praeger boy he smelled like a sick whore; and Schwantz said he then went to the back of the store; for damn sure he wanted no part of that conversation. But after that, there was none, says Schwantz. The Praeger boy put his bean cans and cracker sack in the crook of his arm and, saying nothing, left. Schwantz, fearful in the dark rear of his store, counted his blessings. Then, smack! a damn shot, right through the screen door and into that upright in the rear. Not near to killing anybody, but it had the redhead hiding behind the pickle barrel until Schwantz told him to come out, for God's sake. The shooter, leaving behind a strong fishy smell, was long gone. And, says Pfeiffer, the redhead told Schwantz that if someone dug the slug out of that beam, to save it for him, for his watch fob.

Emil, say I, are you saying Harris took a shot at the redhead, or maybe Schwantz? I cannot see . . .

Now, now, says Pfeiffer. It is not for me to say that he was shooting at somebody—no blood was shed—but he sure did shoot into the store.

Otto speaks up: God knows whose word you are going on, Sheriff, in these accusations about Harris: but you know there are folks around here jealous of us Praegers, what my father has built up here, and that fact rubs some of these buggers who never cleared a dime a year, wrong; and then they say these things.

Yes, Otto, surely people differ, and there are folks hereabouts who might be jealous of your old man—your father, that is—and if you just tell me who they are, and if they been shooting into our public buildings, or even just burning barns and poisoning dogs, why hell, I will pinch them in a minute!

Otto glowers, and Pfeiffer goes on: You know what happens then, if someone is so resentful of your old man? Well, he will not be burning your neighbor's barn, by God, he will burn yours!

Clearly, Pfeiffer grows testy. I say: Now, then, is my whole family to be dragged into this, our good name: You are awfully quick to throw in Harris' name here, and it could be anyone. It could be Clarence Schneider, or Burton—.

Pfeiffer pulls himself up; the little peacock on his shiny perch, managing to puff himself into a larger size, more to that of a man, and a simmering redness comes into his face: he has had enough.

Damn it to hell, Gerhardt, he yells. I can not keep up this play-acting of yours forever. We have known each other for a long time, and I never known you to give a man so much horses--t as now.

Emil, say I, you never came here before with a claim that one of my boys shot at a man.

Ha ha, says Pfeiffer. Go ahead and think of him as a hot gun-slinger, ha ha; but he burned a barn and poisoned them dogs—that is what he has been up to, Gerhardt, your boy.

He huffs and puffs, steaming up the icy air all around his head, and out of that cloud announces: You think you can hide him for long, do you, eh? We will get that son of a bitch of yours, you bet! He aint going nowhere that he can hide from that mark on him. We will fetch him right over to Yankton and put him away for a nice little vacation; you can bet on that, Gerhardt!

He snaps the reins over the rear ends of his little team and turns so tightly his buggy wheels scarcely make the circle, and is off.

IT IS A SAD and silent supper we sit down to; and I think more than one of us is not far short of tears. Her face drawn gray with worry, Ma serves out the cornbread with twitching fingers. . . .

His supper complete, Otto announces: Well he is halfway to Oregon by now; and he goes to the foot of the stairs to pull off his boots, and then up to bed, without another word. And the others go, too; Ma as well, although she does not sleep, I know; putting a match to the lamp on my table here in the corner, I can hear her breathing.

This becomes a most wretched duty, setting down these last events. I am not sure I will do it much anymore. A man must have an appetite for it, or it is only scribbling.

. . . *Halfway to Oregon;* I would say not. I would say to the south and east—the badlands, the sand hills. To go there, I think would be for Harris . . . suitable . . . if he is indeed running; or is he just now dragging back from a Zimmerman debauch and ignorant of all the commotion into which his name has been thrown?

Surely no one under this roof sleeps soundly these nights: perhaps the twins, given the easy ways of youth; but who else? Ma lies most grievously awake: there is near to a sob in the catch of her breathing; and I know her thoughts well enough, for all the years we have lain side by side: Is Harris gone then, too? Is he the second child lost to me, to Gerhardt and me? . . . That first baby taken from us before she had a name, as if she would never be known to the world. But in murmured agreement at her little grave we bestowed upon her a name, her secret name.

And far above in dreamless sleep.
Safe in Christ's tender fold,
Our Esther doth serenely rest,
From winter's chill and cold.

NOV. 3. This is not a frost but a freeze. Ma hauls the last of her geraniums into the back porch, and ice needs breaking in the stock tank where a heifer or two slides her nose in puzzlement across the ice. I put a woolen shirt over my underwear, and doing so, I think that a man in open country, sleeping where he can, will find this very hard weather.

We are at our bacon and eggs, and as she brings her nightclothes to the porch to air, Ma says: You have not banked the house yet. And indeed we have not, with such distractions as have presented themselves.

Yes, yes, says Otto as if he has just been kicked in his hinder; this was not the kind of thing he ever forgot. Me and Henry will do it today. We got that pile of manure we saved west of the barn. We was going to do it, and other things got in the way.

But Ma is at the sink, washing dishes, and does not listen. Otto, watching her bent back, says: We will do it, Ma; we will do it.

NOV. 5. Why I bother to set this down, I hardly know—well, yes, I know; scratching at this page becomes a substitute for sleep, if there is a substitute for such; I think not. But this has been a frozen dreary day, all the drearier in that we have the duty to entertain our neighbor Krupp, who has for some reason dragged along on an old hip-sprung mule one of his snot-nosed brats, who sits sniffling and snuffling deep on his sway-backed mount, while Krupp greets us as if the Queen of England was sending the Praegers best wishes by way of him. I know his good nature to be spurious, and yet it is a small relief to have even that countering the sour glumness which overlays us the past several days.

He too has winter on his mind: She will be a cold one, he says: you seen them sundogs? She will be cold.

Yes, yes, say I: Nor would I be surprised. I have seen some cold summers and some hot ones, and some cold winters, but I have never been privileged to see a hot winter. How about yourself?

He passes over my little speech with a wincing smile. Gerhardt, says he, you know that business over at Beidermann's?

I have heard.

Well, it is a damn shame, aint it? That old boy is up against it now, the time of year being what it is, and him with all that stock, and all his hay gone up—well, he had a little stack off from the barn but it does not amount to beans. Now, what I been thinking— well, I been talking to Schneider and I ran into Willis at the livery day afore yesterday—he was having hisself a little chat with the Widow Jenssen; she was waiting there by the wagon for Beidermann to buy hisself some stuff and, boy, he needs plenty. Well, what Willis says, and I agree with him, is that the both of us, and Schneider is going along, we throw in a few loads of fodder for Beidermann. He got plenty of range, sure, but his cattle sure cannot handle ten feet of snow and ice until next April.

By this time Krupp has found himself a comfortable seat on my porch steps, for all that I have not invited him to do so; and chill as is the air, he has a sufficient layering of tallow to stay warm. He tamps a wad of rough tobacco into his pipe, and in the yard his boy slides off the mule, which stands dead on its feet, as its recent rider shuffles toward the barn to see what the twins, who seem pleased to see him, are up to.

I cannot say I have ever seen Krupp so much at home on my place as he has made himself this cold morning; he is usually a man who shows some deference; but now he has his pipe pulling well and points the stem at me, saying: So what we been talking about, Schneider and me and the other boys, is we get all the folks around here to throw in—you and Johansen, and Laverene if we can get hold of him when he aint in Bismarck trying to finagle something out for himself with the government. Hell, we get eight, ten boys chipping in, and we get Beidermann with them giant animals of his to help haul it, and I do believe we can do it in three, four days, stack it up close against the south side of his house. Everybody come up with a couple or three loads; some of us, a little better off, might chip in more, eh? What do you think, Gerhardt? Half-dozen loads, maybe?

One does well to stay wary of Krupp until he reveals himself fully—if such is possible for him to do. He would like to think himself a tad ahead of the next man, always, unaware that he lacks the wherewithal to bring it off.

Krupp, my friend, say I, you are a man with keen neighborly instincts, as is the admirable Schneider and whoever else you have rung in on this.

Now, above his team, on a rack of the last cornstalks fit for feeding, Otto comes into the yard, draws up and tosses the reins to the twins who move the rack to the side of the barn for unloading.

He comes over, hailing Krupp: How are you, sir?

Krupp replies: Very well, my boy. He waves his pipe stem toward the load the twins are throwing off, and says: I see you are working short-handed, then?

Otto looks to me, uncertain, and I say: We have all we need; and to Otto: Our Mister Krupp here is in the business of collecting hay, to see Mister Beidermann through the winter.

From out his mouth Krupp expels vaporous clouds of the foul weed he burns, through which emission he mutters, True, true, and you will throw in what you can, eh? Gerhardt? Three loads? Four?

Otto, who knows our hay, I might say better than myself, says: Hold on. We got to know where we stand in our own needs. This winter will not be any easier on us than the last, and we aint got that much more hay. Give us a couple weeks of ice holding up a thaw, and we got to bring in our horses, too, and they can go through—

Krupp is as expert at waving his pipe stem as an Old Country conductor is with his baton. Yes, yes, Otto, he says. The winter here aint likely to be much worse than the one at Beidermann's, eh? And there is the other thing you got to work into your figuring—and he is talking to me now, not Otto—which is that Beidermann sure as hell did not bring this business on himself. His barn was *burned,* eh? And he did not light the match which done it; and I would be a lying bastard if I said he was the one poisoned his own dogs, eh? Listen, we got some weather coming, Gerhardt, no squaw winter this year. You remember times we fed cottonwood bark and ground-up cobs? Well, them fine horses of Beidermann will be living off the tarpaper off his house. Help is damn well due him, these being the circumstances . . . and from you, considering. . . .

And he falls silent, a breath short of uttering Harris' name.

He may have his need, sure, says Otto. Everybody does. But I will not be the one to haul hay or anything else to him. He would shoot me the first foot I set on his land.

Krupp knocks out his pipe on the porch step and says: I can see if he will send his team over to pick up—

No, no, say I. Krupp, let me ask you to suppose that it is me bereft of fodder, and you approach Mister Beidermann as you approach me here, cajoling aid for the Praeger benefit. You demand he deliver a half-dozen loads of hay out of his barn, where it is stored for the vital use of his animals, as it is all they will have to keep them alive in freezing weather. What do you suppose he says to your entreaty?

He would surely have to say *yes,* says Krupp and proceeds with a cleverness he has shown little knack for in the past; first I tell him this, that you will be feeding your spring seed to your hens so you have something to boil up for Sunday dinners, up to March, maybe. But your barn and all your hay—gone up. I see you got a little stack of slough hay over there where it did not catch, which will feed your milkers for a while; so you got that much anyways. But now me and Schneider see if we can talk Beidermann into helping out, and he has to think about it. But you see, what eats at him, Gerhardt, which does not eat at you, is another thing—those dead dogs, poisoned. A man hates to see that, and here it is some unknown neighbor sneaks in and tosses some poisoned fish to your dogs, so as to have the time to dump his coal oil aside your barn and get it to burning—

Krupp has taken to grand gesticulation here, like a Baptist minister, vast gestures including all the country-side.

—and when he has got a nice little flame going, he takes himself off down to Schwantz's store and puts a hole in the old man's door. What can a man say about that? Maybe he was shooting at old Schwantz, more likely at that drunk redhead kid and his big mouth; maybe at nothing, who knows? It was cowardly, for all that no blood was shed. But you, Gerhardt, you lost all that hay, and how you gonna get it back? It has got to come from somewhere, and there aint many places where it can. So, Gerhardt, you being the burned-out one, which way you gonna look?

I wave at him to stop. Krupp, say I, I take your point. And I am grateful that nowhere in that burst of eloquence does he inject any names; for the name of Harris is there to be said. Pfeiffer has named him, as has Beidermann: the law and the victim—between them a name is thrown, smeared, into the world.

Krupp, say I, it is getting cold and we have work to do, both of us. You are, I know, by nature, generous, as are all our neighbors, surely. I would propose that I would not be out of place in your company; and yet there are calculations to be made . . . and we shall see.

So be it, Gerhardt, says Krupp, and tucks his pipe into his shirt pocket with its dottle-stained bottom half; and hollers to his kin at the rope-swing, taking turns with the twins, to get his hind-end onto that mule quick, as they have a two-hour ride and a mess of calves to feed before the old dog barks. . . . Now, this last sounds more like the Krupp we know; not the one trying to balance loads of hay on the head of a pin.

They are well gone when Otto says: They aint getting that hay.

It is not *they,* say I; it is *he;* and we shall see.

No, it is *they,* says Otto; Krupp and Schneider and Willis and Laverene—which is one little bastard can make trouble all the way to Yankton—that gang is against us, Pa; you know it too. Hell, hay will never be enough—it will be oats and corn and come spring, you gonna give him our seed too? He aint the only one got bad luck. If he cannot handle a little trouble here, let him run back East to his folks, like all those others.

Yes, Otto, say I, you have got some fine contrarian spunk in you, but facts are facts. Our Beidermann came out of Canada, and to run to his folks, why, he would go north, not east. And as for his folks, my feeling is he has few. Right from the beginning, he has been a solitary man.

Well, then, says our stubborn oldest son, let him take up with that Jenssen woman—they been so thick. Hell, he put up half her hay, after he run off that drunk tramp she hired who harnessed her team crosswise and damn near crippled the mare. Let her help him feed his stock. He sure done enough for her. . . .

IT IS AFTER SUPPER and the boys go off to pick their teeth on the porch, where Ma will soon bring them sugar cookies. Otto, staying put, mutters his opinions still: after all, he has rights that he knows are his, nor would I gainsay him here. Around us, at one of their lesser chores, the twins clear the supper table, and listen for a word favoring their hero and mentor—having heard slurs and vilification enough—for all that it is he who maligns the name of their blood brother, and with what probity? To be sure, with his needling, teasing, and nudging, Harris is less than the perfect brother, but that is the way of boys.

The two tag along as I take my nightly visit to the little house. Free of the older boys talking over them, they scurry beside me through the weeds that flank the well-worn path; they are near as tall as I am now, and squeaky voiced.

Says one: We could do it, Pa, the two of us. Load up whatever you say—that old bunch of stuff from the bog, we can take that. We can haul it over there ourselves, with Prince and Maude.

Says the other, with a look over his shoulder: He might shoot Otto, but he will not shoot us.

My hand is on the wooden latch and I say: You boys get out of here. I have some figuring to do before anybody does anything.

Through the closed door I hear them mutter as they scuff down the path . . . That old hay aint worth nothing anyway. . . and back to the house, disappointed.

.   .   .

THEY SLEEP NOW, I trust, the disappointed little ones. Who else dares sleep I venture not to say; Otto, perhaps, in respite from his anger and disgust; but sleep comes hard to those baffled and soured by disappointment, and worry; which I make trivial by setting these words so easily on this page when they should be chiseled upon alabaster slabs of a weight to match the heaviness they lay upon our souls.

Where is Harris, then? In the blink of an eye he is gone; how can that be? And why Harris—the fifth son—and not Otto, Cornelius, Henry, August, the twins? Why has not one or two or all of them gone amiss, if it is in the world for that to happen to any one of them. It can worry a man forever. . . . Yes, of them all, then which one? He is the one marked; and indeed, it is myself and Wilhemina, the two of us, who put that mark on him. . . . Old Doc Yost, in his last year, growling out of the corner of his mouth as he wiped his hands: Well, he got a splotch up here under his chin; birthmark is what it is; nothing important; we see them like that from time to time.

One of the boys tending the loose cattle with a freighter that came through Zimmerman in mid-December was telling the pair of idlers warming their feet in the livery barn that if it was work they wanted, Big John Knudsen was hiring down at Quail Lake. Harris was helping old Voight bring in a load of last year's prairie hay, and overheard.

"He's got hisself a big bunch of hosses," said the boy, a little redheaded Irish kid. "Homely buggers, I'll tell you. He's feeding 'em rotten spuds out there on the ice."

To get these nags to auction, said the kid, Big John wanted hands. The loungers looked the other way, but Harris figured this might be his chance to get moving.

For two months he had holed up working at Voight's Big Hoss Livery, the Voight who owned it being old Jim Voight's mother, who looked to be a hundred and two, and ordered her bachelor son around like a rented mule. She was softer with Harris, though, calling him "m'boy," and put him up for found and two bits handed him here and there, and saw to it that he had an extra wool army blanket when he moved into the helper's stall afront of the horses' stalls. It was comfortable enough and he didn't have to share it with two big snoring brothers: a good cot, a wash-stand, a clean basin and slop bucket, and even a bar of soap in an old sardine can with nail holes in the bottom. But no lamps al-lowed amidst all that hay, so when the sun went down, Harris took a stroll down the road to the Sand Hill Saloon and sat around with an old boy or two listening to the wild stories spun at the bar; once or twice, he'd had cash enough to buy a shot to keep his standing.

The horses at Quail Lake set him to figuring. He didn't want to vex old Voight by mentioning beforehand that he had a chance at a better job; so he quietly packed up his stuff, including a nice buffalo robe that someone had apparently forgotten under the cot: nobody had said he couldn't have it, so he rolled it as tightly as he could and jammed it under the gear in back of his horse's saddle, putting nearly a camel's hump onto the animal.

The old bay had had a few good weeks, hardly ridden and standing in clean straw out of the weather, stuffing himself with the timothy that it was Harris' job to dig out of the high snow-covered stacks that stood on the acre or so of land behind the sta-bles. He did a good day's work; he didn't figure anybody was shortchanged by his leaving so soon.

It wasn't quite light, the frigid sky more black than not, when he had all his gear laced up, ready to leave. From the house next door, where he lived with his mother, old Voight came out to unlock the stable for business. He seemed unsurprised to find Harris standing there with a packed horse.

"Up early," he said.

Harris mumbled awkwardly: some stuff had come up . . . hadn't been time. Much obliged to Voight for the job and all . . .

Jim Voight looked him up and down. "Shit, you going off with John Knudsen and them hosses, ain't you?

Harris shrugged.

"Well, you a grown boy," said Voight. "Gonna do what the hell you please. Me, I did dumb things too, when I was your age. Just remember that you working for Big John Knudsen."

People like to call him Big Yawn, said Voight, and it was a familiar name hereabouts, last heard two, three years ago when he went bust on two sections of mortgaged land near Buford. What the drought didn't get of his wheat, people said, the cutworms got of his corn. People thought he had disappeared east to his wife's folks, but here he was, turned up again like a bad penny, running some gypsy horse-trading operation out on Quail Lake.

"Ask yourself this," said Voight. "Where'd he get all them hosses? And you can bet there's a sheriff or two in this end of the country who'd like to know the answer to that too. Just make sure, m'boy, that you don't end up getting handed your own ass."

Harris murmured that he wouldn't, and as he pulled himself onto his encumbered horse, Grandma Voight came from her house, waving to him. "Harold," she said—it was what he'd told them he was called—"wait a bit." She handed up to him a paper-wrapped package the size of a couple of sandwiches. "Here's some eats, Harold, and God bless you." It was as if she'd had this ready hours ago, knowing.

Harris fumbled the package; he could scarcely whisper his thanks; and he could not kick the old bay out of there fast enough; and he hoped to God she hadn't seen the buffalo robe jammed under his gear.

WITH SO MUCH FRESH SNOW, the old bay was knee-deep nearly all the way, out of town, down the road and over the bluff into the lake basin, dead tired when Harris pulled him up in the late afternoon and looked over what was spread before him.

That kid on the bull train was right—Knudsen had himself a bunch of horses. In the snow-covered landscape, they were massed everywhere. Bands of a few dozen longhaired nags huddled here and there in the draws and on the lee side of the low hills, where the snow was less deep. Some stood unmoving, their heads hanging, and others pawed the snow to get at what little frozen grass they could find: the dirty spots they had already worked over covered the slopes down to the lake like scabs. Several grubby men on horseback who looked to have been recruited from the ice-cutters or the coots who trapped muskrats at the lake plodded along the outskirts of the loose animals to keep them from scattering. The really ornery-looking broncs, he saw, were in makeshift wire-and-rope corrals along the road where it ran past the lake.

It was a while before Harris took in the whole sight. How in hell, in the dead of winter, could Knudsen afford to feed all these critters? He had to be better off than anyone gave him credit for.

He found Big John in his headquarters, a ten-by-ten sod hut at the south end of the lake. In person, he belied his name, being a medium-sized man. He wore small eyeglasses which glinted in the light of his kerosene lantern, and he peered at Harris in a shrewd way as they shook hands and Harris offered his name: "Harold," and said he'd heard there might be a job here.

"Yup, you got it right," Big John said; he was indeed hiring a few top-notch boys to accompany these fine animals out of Dakota over to the Iowa border, where, through privileged knowledge passed on by his Kansas City partners, he had been apprised of a prime market for quality horseflesh. Everybody was wanting good horses these days, Knudsen explained; did Harold know that? The army was buying, the freight companies were buying, the express lines were buying; and by God, even sight-seers from the East—Englishmen from England, for example—were buying up the best horses for their Western tours and excursions. The Goddamned nobility were coming out to shoot buffalo and prairie chickens and were hollering for horses. How were they gonna take their expensive tours without horses? They were crying for horses back there. Just yesterday Knudsen had gotten a wire message from New York—*Ship more horses.* It was, he trusted Harold would see, a cinch sellers' market all the way. A blind man could make money! A man who didn't know a horse's head from its ass could make money. Harold didn't know how lucky he was to get in on this extraordinary venture.

Having presented Harris with these facts, Knudsen drew a sober face. "By God," he said, "don't I wish I could make this trip with you boys? Nothing I like more than riding a good horse across that prairie. Buffalo, antelope, rabbit, chicken—you can shoot enough meat in an hour to feed an army." Four hundred miles of cold and snow and storms? Hell, he said, he couldn't count the times he'd done that as a young man, no older than Harold was today.

He shook his head sadly. "But I ain't the man I was, and I admit it. Nope, them glory days is gone for Big John. Goddamn back give out on me, wouldn't you know? A man like myself, too."

Well, there was one bright spot in all this—the way his biggest boy, Cobb, had come along. A hell of a youngster. If anybody could fill Big John's shoes when it came to horses, it was that fine lad, Cobb. Maybe Harold was acquainted with him; they weren't that far apart in years?

Harris shook his head.

He'd hired eight men, Knudsen announced. Harold would be number nine. And now that he was signing on—he was, wasn't he?—they'd leave at four o'clock tomorrow morning. The pay, Knudsen had to admit, was damned generous—a dollar a day and plenty to eat. Harold would surely recognize that was above prevailing rates. Cash money paid no later than the day following their delivery of the horses at Dakota City.

They shook hands on it, and Big John said Harold could sleep in the headquarters. Cobb would wake him in the morning. He took the lantern when he left, and in the cold dark on a bag of cornhusks, Harris fell asleep full of misgivings. But still, this venture would put him on the move, which, he figured, was wise; and when a hand poked him awake in the black of night, he was ready to go.

Saying no more than "We're set," Cobb stood by as he rolled up his gear. In the dark, Harris tried to size him up. He was tall and thin, no more than a half-dozen years older than Harris, and from what Harris could see as they came out of the hut onto the snowy path, looked stooped and pale, as if he wasn't any healthier than he had to be. Maybe bad backs ran in that family, like beaked noses did in his.

STEADILY THEY GOT UNDER WAY. Big John collared Cobb where the old freight road came around the lake, and pumped a loud stream of instructions at him. Cobb sat his horse silently, staring at the snow and nodding. Harris pulled the old bay over a few yards to where two riders sat their horses, half-listening to Knudsen, waiting to get moving. Harris said, "I guess you boys are in on this drive too."

"I guess we are," said one. He was an Indian boy not much older than Harris who said folks generally called him Chief. The other rider, a boy of about seventeen, leaned over to shake Harris' mittened hand. He was a broad-shouldered fellow, his face hardly visible in the pulled-up hood. His name was Duwayne. He said he was from near Zimmerman, but Harris couldn't remember seeing him before.

Having laid out the marching orders to Cobb, Knudsen called over to Harris and Duwayne, "Now, I want you two boys to take up the back side here. Cobb's gonna head 'em out." He motioned to Chief to follow him, and told them he'd ride along for a mile or two, despite the misery in his back, and get them over the toughest spots. The muskratters were chasing band after band out of the ravines and off the hillsides, and others sprang the ropes and wires of the corrals. A mass of brown and gray and earth-colored horseflesh surged around and past Harris and Duwayne, who pulled up their mounts and watched the horses merge into a herd, with Knudsen and Chief funneling them on, Harris supposed, to Cobb and the other riders hidden far ahead. As the last horses came dashing up, Harris and Duwayne fell in behind. In front of them, the horses slewed and vaulted for footing, plunging through drifts that obscured the road. Someone yelled, "Wahoo! Yippee! Git along!" It was Big John, hastening back to headquarters. The muskratters fell back, too, one scruffy old geezer saluting as the old bay lugged past; the only good-bye Harris had gotten so far.

A MIST OF SLEET began to fall as the horizon lightened. It looked to Harris as if they were on a slab of tableland with nothing in their way for a day or two until the river breaks. Riding in the rear, he was ten or twelve rods from Duwayne, but often they ranged close enough to talk. Chief was halfway up the herd on the south flank, with Cobb and the others too far ahead to see.

The sleet, having wetted him enough to freeze, stopped. It grew fully light, cold and gray. The air snapped in Harris' nostrils. The mass of horses was strung way back, a half-dozen animals wide; he couldn't see more than ten rods down the line. With the light of day on them, the animals nearest revealed a bothersome shabbiness and a sense of ill-health. But no doubt the pride of the herd was up front.

Duwayne angled his horse toward him across the trail of smashed and dirtied snow. "What d'ya think of these fiddleheads?" he called. "See any you'd like to take home to the old lady?"

"I don't know," said Harris. "Knudsen said he was gonna sell 'em to Englishmen for their excursions."

Duwayne hooted. "You bet," he said. "Some swell in fancy britches is gonna slap his little pancake saddle on *that*?" He pointed to a skinny, hammer-headed gray mare, her loose belly hanging, thick winter hair sticking out at angles and scabbed with snow, and one chewed ear cocked wrong. She wasn't much worse than her nearest companions, all sickle-hocked and roach-backed. They all seemed unusually small to Harris. Pa wouldn't waste hay on a one of them.

"It's all wild range stock, bunch of pig-eyed nags," Duwayne said. "They ain't had nothing to eat, and their mamas and daddies was all bred wrong anyways. Hell, they been hungry all their lives. Old Knudsen couldn't afford to feed 'em, so he has to ship 'em. Nobody who knows his business would do that in the middle of winter."

Harris found that none of this came as a surprise. But yet he thought that surely there was *some* market for these culls. Knudsen wasn't sending them off with only a hope and prayer: he couldn't be fool enough to expect any horse trader in the country to pay more than a nickel for these woeful goats.

"They're canners, is my guess," Duwayne said. "Going straight to the Ioway butchers and get made into some nice horse steaks for the foreigners. Plenty of 'em eat horse meat, you know—Frenchies, Chinamen. Hell, they'd rather have that than deer or beef."

Duwayne pulled his horse over to let a couple of jack-spavined stragglers get by, and Harris sought to appraise the truth in what he'd said. No good reason to doubt it. He'd heard tales about Frenchmen. This herd might be headed straight for their tables. For sure, no one hereabouts would eat them. He had a vague notion that there was a law in the States about white men eating horse or dog meat, unless they were dying from starvation. Hell, then folks even ate their kids. But such a law wouldn't hold back a Frenchman.

Still, he wondered if the top-notch animals, all the trim express horses and big freight brutes weren't up front being coddled by the other riders, and because he and Duwayne were the youngest, they got the scrubs to tend.

BY MIDDAY THE HERD was moving forward fairly well. The animals in the rear had the easiest time, the snow having been trampled into the semblance of a rough trail. Harris' bay followed on this threshed-over road, scattered with dung and yellow holes burned all the way to the ground beneath, here and there rimmed with red from bloody urine. Both Harris and Duwayne kept busy shooing back broncs that drifted to the side, testing their chances for escape. Later in the day, Harris caught up with Chief and complained.

"We could use another hand or two back here," he said. "A lot of these buggers keep wanting to go home."

"Sure enough," said Chief. The big collar of his coat was turned up, hugging his chin like wings. Outside it hung an elk's eye-tooth on a string. A length of old towel was tied under his chin and over his ears. "We sure oughta have more than just us. I think Cobb's gonna hire some, if he can. I think his old man told him to."

"Well, hell," Harris said. "He told me he had nine guys."

Chief looked at him to see if he was joking. "Nope," he said, waving a mitten back toward Duwayne. "There's just us."

. . .

BY THE SECOND DAY, the herd was moving in fits and starts as the horses dropped back to paw the snow in hope of fodder. Sometimes, to spare his old horse, Harris walked, tramping through hillocks of flailed snow dotted with horse apples. He marked anew the scruffiness of the knee-sprung specimens just ahead. Most hardly came to his shoulder. All appeared to carry scant eating meat. He hoped to God Big John wasn't working some slimy hoax and everybody would get cheated out of their wages, and then the law got mixed up in it. That made him uneasy. That morning he had asked Cobb if there was any doubt about selling the herd, and Cobb, who was a lot more nervous than a boss should be, had jumped on him and told him to just drive the bastards and leave the financial angles to somebody else.

Besides being boss, it turned out that Cobb was also the cook—at least, he said he'd do the cooking, but all that meant was he'd get a fire going at nightfall and haul out beans, bacon, and canned tomatoes from the sacks on the two packhorses he was trailing. Then he'd tell his tiny crew to heat up what they wanted.

Some cook, thought Harris at supper, gnawing the half-done bacon he'd heated in the pan he'd made by cutting the bottom inch off a three-pound lard can. At least they had plenty of coffee, and he made it as hot as he could stand, for the warmth in it.

Even with the promised nine men, he saw, it would have been a short crew. He judged they had more like three hundred head, not two hundred as Big John had said, spread out for a mile, with stragglers stretching it even farther. Finding feed would take up a lot of time, he realized, and unless there was no snow up ahead, the heavy going could tack a few days onto their trip. . . . He calculated how his wages would add up if they didn't bring these nags to market before the middle of January.

Nobody broached the subject of the missing six hands with Cobb. It was as if they should have known better. They each had their job, Cobb and Duwayne now on the front flanks, Chief and Harris at the rear; trailing behind, they kept an eye out for likely ponies, hoping to spell their own tired mounts. Chief owned a lariat, with which he demonstrated a deft hand on a laggard bundle of bones, but they saw nothing they cared to ride.

This was the coldest country Harris had ever been in. A man might think he'd seen colder, coming from so far north, but he hadn't. Nights, trying to sleep, all the furthest parts of him turned tingling or numb, as if about to fall off. When he managed to doze, he'd start up in alarm, feeling his toes like stones. He had two good army blankets and Voight's fine buffalo robe. Substantial as these were, they didn't go far enough in cold like this; and even though Harris knew this to be true, it didn't prevent him from making a grave mistake.

It happened near a little iced-over gully Chief said was called Biscuit Creek. Here they came upon a pair of mixed-bloods— brothers, they claimed—traveling on mules out of Nebraska to Bismarck, where they said their father owned a saloon. A shifty pair who inspired no confidence at all, Harris feared that Cobb might offer them jobs. But Cobb had no such intention: he had his crew; and when he turned his back and rode off, they looked to the other boys, hoping for some advantage out of this encounter. They had a jug, produced with a bit of show worthy of its value, and allowed both Harris and Duwayne a sample direct from the jug's frigid lip.

Chief watched these goings-on without pleasure, and waved them off in disgust when the smarmiest of the two suggested he might wish to swap that elk's tooth for this jug of fine rye whiskey. The penniless Duwayne, when they looked at him, only shrugged unhappily.

But Harris nudged his horse in closer. "Hold on," he said, feeling an uplift in his spirits, a sense of something pleasant ready to happen, that he hadn't known for months.

He showed them what he had to offer, and of course only the buffalo robe would do. But Harris, for all his desire to close the deal, balked; the robe really wasn't his, he said, at the same time thinking—well, if they insisted. . . .

They settled for one of his woolen blankets, the best one, unfrayed, without holes. Harris lashed the jug handle to his saddle horn; he felt easier for having it, and the damned blowing snow seemed less bothersome.

THE REST OF THAT DAY, they followed the creek—which soon took a slight bend and became a frozen river, bearing south toward Severance, scalloped drifts along the bank. The wind-swept ice was easier going for the horses, although many stepped awkwardly, slipping from the snow balls packed into their hooves. In most places, the ice was a yard thick, but there were honeycombed stretches too, and rubber ice, and then a thin spot claimed a few ponies on the side of the herd away from Harris. He heard Duwayne yelling like a madman, but didn't see them go, or even the break in the ice. He moved closer to his own bank, though, his heart beating as fast as when he'd turned his back on Beidermann's barn.

All week the wind hadn't stopped once. It might calm a little after dark, but whipped up again during the day. That afternoon it picked up suddenly. In ten minutes it was no longer a fierce, bucketing blast from the west, but had boiled into a murderous, screaming gale tearing out of the northwest full of snow—horizontal streaks of snow, the wind too violent to let the flakes fall.

Not long before, Harris had been thinking that cold though it was, they'd been lucky with weather. Now he couldn't see the horse's ass in front of him, and he soon grew uneasily aware that for all the wind and snow so far, only now was he about to get the feel of them joined in a way to guarantee his and all mankind's misery. He pulled his hood tight and kept a firm hand on the bay's left rein, to keep him from swinging his tail square to the storm.

Under all this weather, Cobb didn't wait until dark before he pulled the herd away from the river and onto a long plateau slanting off a ridge, which the wind had cleared enough for the animals to get at a little frozen bunch grass.

With Chief's help, Harris found the only half-protected spot to be seen in the roiling snow. It was a little stand of stunted cedars, shoulder-high, but with gnarled branches making a partial low roof, under which they threw their bedrolls. Fifty feet away, hardly a shadow through the snow, Duwayne scooped a trench in the snow alongside a downed cottonwood trunk, well out of the wind.

Harris was hacking the ice out of the bay's hooves with his knife when Cobb emerged carrying their supper food. With difficulty they got a small fire started under the cedars and quickly ate.

As Cobb and Duwayne left to ride the first night shift—Harris and Chief to take the second—Cobb called back. "Watch yourself," he said. He had been distracted all the while they hunkered over the fire eating, peering first in one direction and then another into the screen of snow. "A guy can get lost in this stuff."

Chief called after him, "*I* know that, Boss. You tell your horses that."

HARRIS HUNKERED UNDER the cedar boughs, numb and dismayed. He had tied his horse in close, hoping to get its bulk between him and at least the worst of the storm; but the miserable animal had backed itself into the blowing snow and was little help. But he had the buffalo robe and the one blanket; and he had the jug, and the knowledge that it was at hand buoyed him. With some difficulty, he got the robe worked up behind him, against the buffeting wind, then struggled to tuck his wool blanket around his lower half, but in the effort hauled in considerable snow under the blanket. This, he could see, would be as miserable a night as God could wish upon him.

But he had his jug, and the first pull always warmed; he knew that from his slim experience; but how many more you had to take to get you feeling better, he wasn't sure. He tried a few: they were a great help.

A sluggish notion that someone was kicking his boots brought him halfway back to sensibility. It was Duwayne, trying to get his relief rider onto his feet.

Chief, half out of sight, yelled, "C'mon, Harold, let's go; whole bunch of sunshine up ahead."

With difficulty, Harris flopped himself out of his snow-crusted wraps. When he was free, on his knees in the snow, he fumbled to find the jug. It was like ice against his lips, but turned gloriously warm going down; and as he savored this he made sure the cork was tight.

But when he got himself ready for duty, he couldn't see a yard in any direction. "Where's them damn horses?" he yelled, and Chief, nearly invisible himself, hollered back, "They're out there somewheres, by God. I doubt a man could miss the bastards, if you know how to follow turds."

Then he disappeared.

Harris felt more than cold, and needed three tries to heave himself onto his old bay, who sagged under him as if this was the last straw, but managed to straighten out as his rider secured the jug on the horn, after a satisfying pull.

Now, where was the herd? Where was Chief? Where the hell was anything? And how did you get a horse moving through the fucking snow that was up to his eyebrows? The old bay pushed along not too badly, figured Harris, taking a good slug from his jug, and it crossed his mind that neither the unhappy critter nor his benumbed rider had any idea where the hell they were. If there were horses out there, Harris didn't see them; and it crossed his mind, as he worked the cork out of the jug one more time, that they might have gone off in some other direction. There sure as hell was no sign of the bastards hereabouts. Shit, he told himself, this ain't gonna work. . . .

But whatever sharp whiskey scent came off Harris' jug from his frequent uncorking of it didn't bother the old bay's instincts: his cold nose picked up something good up ahead, and that's the way he went, although with difficulty; and soon Harris was encouraged to catch a glimpse of Chief, like a shadow seen through a screen door, but all in white. Then he disappeared again.

Harris untangled the jug's tie from the saddlehorn and had a warming nip as he stared into the swirling whiteness; he knew that however perky *he* felt, his pony was worn way down, and the snow was only getting deeper. Soon the old nag took a few flailing steps backward and stopped dead, belly-deep, shooting out his breath like a blacksmith's bellows. Harris knew what was called for here, and he considered it as the snow plastered itself to him top to bottom: he needed to get off his ass and plow a trail up front for the weary beast; and as he figured the degree of nastiness in such an undertaking, he went to the jug again.

This ain't working at all, he thought. No horses, no crew, snow up to your neck, and cold enough to freeze a fella's dinger off. Shit.

He crawled off his horse, waist-deep in snow on what seemed to be the downslope of a gentle draw; and before he took this easier way, he floundered about in front of his horse to see if the snow revealed any trace of the herd's path. Finding none, he grabbed firm hold of the bay's bridle strap—if the damn nag couldn't carry him above the snow, he'd drag him through it.

They had threshed downslope for only a few minutes when Harris found himself stumbling through low growths of willow and alder—perhaps a creek bed was buried near.

He had his arm bent before his face when he stumbled smack into a wall of creek-side brush. It rose above his head and was mostly thick-growing, but he found a spot where he could burrow in so that the branches, twigs, really, hindered the snow from blasting full force upon him. Onto what he hoped was a firm growth of willow and not a piece of reed, he tied the old gelding, and dragged his robe and blanket and jug into his little hole; and having managed to work the robe and blanket, now full of snow, around him, he reclined, shivering from head to toe, and took full measure from his jug. . . . And again . . .

A FAINT TRACERY OF LIGHT through the blown snow, and day began; and with it Cobb on his big mare that plowed through drifts where most animals would flounder. Duwayne followed, Chief keeping check on the tail end of the herd as the other two backtracked looking for Harris. The blasting wind sometimes kept Duwayne from catching his breath, but didn't stop Cobb from loud complaints. He alone—no help from his hired hands—had kept the whole damned herd from getting blown away, hadn't slept a goddamned wink. Did a man have to do everything himself? His frozen breath plastered the wolf-fur trim on his hood.

"Where the hell is Harold?" Cobb yelled.

Duwayne didn't bother to answer.

Cobb went on, "We gotta get these critters moving on to some browse, some brush or willows or something. Some of 'em look like they'll drop in a minute."

Duwayne wondered that he hadn't noticed that a week ago.

But Cobb sounded as if he knew where they were, and as the light grew through the screen of snow, east was where it was supposed to be, and Cobb indeed had them pointed in the right direction. "Where the hell is that guy?" he said again. "Go find that bastard."

"What the hell?" said Duwayne. "I don't know." But he pulled his horse around and headed back down the threshed-over snow, dotted with horse apples and yellow holes rapidly filling in. He had little hope, but he thought he remembered where he had last seen Harold, and although that spot looked exactly like every six-foot-deep drift, damned if he didn't catch sight of a little some-thing—a small trench going down-slope; and when he pushed his horse to plow its way down, it nearly bumped into the rear end of the old bay before Duwayne saw it. Then he thought, Jesus, the old nag froze to death right on his feet, like a statue. Even when the horse moved its head a bare inch, he still wasn't sure it was alive; But he dismounted and pushed his way to where the bay was tied and the mound of snow with a head-sized breathing hole.

To Duwayne this didn't look right at all. "Ho, Harold," he called. "Harold . . . ?" He cocked an ear toward the hole, not certain what was down there.

Then the mound moved, and the blankets beneath it heaved, dislodging some of the snow. Duwayne heard a grunt and a groan, and as more snow fell aside, he saw Harris try to prop himself on an elbow, only half succeeding; knitted hat covering his face to the bridge of his nose and coat collar turned up over chin and cheeks. Out of this poked his hawkish nose, dead white. His legs kicked once or twice against the wrapped blankets and sent more snow flying; but then he abandoned hope of rising, and lay quiet, under the snow.

Duwayne swung off his pony, sinking nearly to his hips, and reached for Harris, pulling back the cap. Harris' eyes were half open, his eyebrows thick with frost. He whispered, "G'wan."

The empty jar lay under the snow at his side. Duwayne kicked it, but it moved hardly an inch in its frozen bed. "You dumb asshole," he said, and picked up the top blanket and shook the snow out of it. It was hard with frozen piss, and cracked as he threw it aside. Under this, Harris was rolled in his buffalo robe, mostly frozen around him, from which his boots stuck out, with his pants leg stiff and shiny with ice. Duwayne didn't want to think what the feet in those boots looked like. Near Harris' head the falling snow quickly covered a brown stain of recent vomit, and the smell of alcohol in it rose sharply in the frozen air.

"Hey, Harold!" Duwayne bent down. "Can you stand up? Can you walk?" But he saw slim prospects of either. "C'mon, get up!"

For a moment, Duwayne looked down at the stupefied face, the blistering cheeks, the pearl-white nose on which the falling snow still melted. This guy was a grown man, or nearly, a year or two further down the road than Duwayne; but if this was where the wisdom of experience took a man, God help the sorry lot of them.

Duwayne leaned down and flipped the snow-stiffened robe and blanket to cover Harris. "I'm gonna get Cobb," he said. "We gotta get you a horse. That nag of yours is shot. Gotta get your drunk ass outta here."

COBB WOULDN'T LEAVE THE HERD, or whatever part of it he had managed to find. He was frantic about getting out of this storm in decent shape—in *any* shape—and already he had lost no telling how many head: enough for the old man to skin him alive. He half-listened to a part of Duwayne's story, and then yelled, "The son of a bitch'll just have to catch up! That's it. We ain't gonna wait!" His shrill voice emerged from the oval into which his hood was drawn, leaving just enough space for his mouth and nose and—if he tipped his head back—his eyes.

Chief, having listened to Duwayne, wheeled his pony toward the herd and disappeared.

Cobb, too, was heading back toward the herd. "Wait a minute," Duwayne called. "What we gonna do with him?"

"Goddamn it," yelled Cobb over his shoulder, "if he's drunk, he ain't gonna get paid for today either!"

He was gone, and Duwayne started after him, but at that moment Chief reappeared out of the snow, towing a thin, high-legged horse, a gelding with more muscle and size than the others, and bearing a sign or two of a harness, tolerant of the hackamore Chief had on him.

"Okay, then," said Chief. "Let's go get that dumb fucker."

But when they came to haul him groaning out of his pit, he was barely conscious. "Come on, Whiskey Boy," said Chief, getting his shoulder under Harris' weight as if he had done this before; Duwayne held the gelding. "You can handle this bronc, fancy rider like you."

"We gotta get his saddle," Duwayne said; but wherever the storm had blown the old bay, it was out of their sight and Harris would have to go saddleless.

He flopped like a fish, but they hoisted him onto the anxious gelding's slim back; he slid from side to side, the horse shying abortively in the deep drifts.

Chief said, "Shit, we'll tie him on," and used his rope to do so. They set out to catch the herd.

Snubbed across his unhappy mount's back, Harris racked with convulsions, began to retch. Right on his tail, Duwayne was at first concerned and then disgusted. He'd never thought he would side with the boss, but as for some drunk getting paid, he could see Cobb's point of view in this matter.

THROUGH THE BLOWING SNOW, the herd was never in sight, but its trail was plain. Some of Big John's fine specimens might have gone through the ice or strolled off into the storm, but a sufficient number remained to leave a filthy, churned-up track, even as the falling snow worked to clean it up.

Before long, Chief stopped and, with Duwayne, checked on the condition of the third man in their crew.

"That rope might be cutting off the blood in his arm there," said Duwayne. Chief shifted Harris and tied a couple of new knots. Harris was virtually lashed to the sorrel's neck. The collar of his coat, vomited upon, had frozen to his cheeks, and Duwayne pried the cloth partly free.

"Don't you pass out no more," Chief said. "'Less you wanna fall and get your head stepped on."

"He gotta be froze down to his ass," said Duwayne, wonderingly.

"If he's cold, he oughtta say so," said Chief, kicking the gouts of snow off his pants and re-mounting. "He sure smells like shit, don't ya, Whiskey Boy?"

"Where's he from?" said Duwayne. "He got folks around here?"

"Couldn't say," said Chief. "Big John took him on at Quail Lake, I think."

They were ready to turn back into the storm.

"You think that was poisoned whiskey?" Duwayne asked.

"Forty-rod hooch? said Chief. "You bet. Uncle of mine up around Mott used to mix up that shit. Traded it to the soldiers. Hell, he put in pepper, gunpowder, anything—a pinch of wolf bait. It didn't have enough kick otherwise."

"I had a little taste back there," Duwayne said. "It didn't seem so bad."

"Didn't, huh?" said Chief. "So you're next."

Heavy snow had almost filled in the herd's trail; while it could still be seen, they plunged after it.

LATER, MAYBE MID-AFTERNOON, they saw Cobb again. Incredibly, the snow had picked up—where in hell was it all coming from?— and the wind came in at new angles as if seeking out one it hadn't tried yet. It seemed to Duwayne to come out of some other coun try, far to the north.

Cobb had calmed a little. "I got 'em settled down up ahead," he said. "There's a little open spring and some bare ground. It's all salt or mineral or something, but they put their noses right into it. We'll let 'em be."

He looked carefully at Harris, roped insensibly to the rangy horse's neck, but said nothing to him. After handing Duwayne the food sack, he went back to keep tabs on "the leaders," as he put it—which were horses Duwayne had never set eyes on. Leaders. He wondered what they looked like.

Chief threshed his way to Harris' horse. "Hey, Mr. Whiskey Harold, you still alive?" He slapped him on his rear, untied the ropes, and when Harris slid off the horse, kept him halfway on his feet and asked, "How about a little whiskey drink right now, eh?"

"Drag him over here," Duwayne called. He had kicked away or stamped down the snow in a wedge-shaped declivity beside a shoulder-high rock. It made a little corner out of the wind. Harris groaned as they lowered him into it.

But even down low, the wind whipped the snow around to sting like nettles. Duwayne retrieved the blanket and buffalo robe from Harris' horse and tossed them to him, where they lay jumbled across his body, gathering snow. With some snatches of chaparral and dry bark he had saved, Duwayne got a sketchy fire burning with scant heat at Harris' feet; the rock, much higher than their heads as they crouched, made a decent heat reflector. Chief, ranging nearby, stumbled over a sizeable cottonwood branch and dragged it in. He kicked the slabs of snow off it and said, "She'll be good for all night, if we can get her started."

With their backs against the wind and protecting the fire, Harris opposite, Duwayne and Chief rustled through the food sack, producing a sheet of dried deer meat and biscuits, a stub of frozen salt pork and a can of tomatoes, also frozen. Duwayne punched a hole in the can with his knife and leaned it with great care close to the little flame, which darted wildly in the wind. On the odd chance that he could get some snow boiling over this unreliable fire, Chief pulled a few paper twists of coffee from the bag and tucked them in his shirt pocket.

Duwayne did his best to wrap the blanket and robe around Harris who, mumbling a protest, did nothing to help; a dead and smelly weight. Having done what he could, Duwayne nudged Harris' snow-caked boots closer to the fire, which had picked up a bit, but then wondered if that was right. If this guy was half as frozen as he looked, he was going to smart something awful when the thaw set in.

A HALF-FROZEN SUPPER in his belly, Duwayne went to untie his bedroll from his saddle, and it was then that Cobb came dashing up like a white phantom out of the snow-filled dark. His big mare threw up snow with her flexed forelegs, half burying the little fire, as Cobb pulled her up.

"Get on them horses right now!" he yelled. He'd reacquired his panic of the morning. "The bastards took off again!"

He sounded to Duwayne like an old woman yelling at her hogs, and he was pulling his poor mare all wrong; she missed stepping on Harris' legs by inches.

"Christ Almighty," said Chief. But he was first on his horse and headed out as confidently as if he knew what needed to be done to repair whatever ruin Cobb had brought. Now Cobb was right behind him, yelling back, "Hey you, Harold! You ain't drawing wages to lay around no goddamned fire! Get your horse!"

Harris, under the snow, made no response.

Cobb was still hollering, now at Chief, far ahead, now at Duwayne, beside him. "They headed south, the whole Goddamn bunch!" Duwayne looked to where he pointed, thinking, well, that might be south; how was a man to know in this shitty storm?

"We gonna head 'em off," yelled Cobb. "C'mon, you follow me." His mare plunged into the obscuring snow.

Duwayne set his pony to follow. The fire had barely started to warm him, and now his cheeks burned again with the cold. He'd taken the food bag and stuffed it into his oilcloth saddle pouch before he realized he'd left nothing for Harold. And now he had to hurry forward to keep from losing Cobb and Chief. But he would come back here soon, or someone would, to get Harold. He tried to fix this spot in his mind, but it was all snow—a big rock, and blowing snow.

Wintry Silence, and a Sudden Moth

❀

⟹ 1888 ⟸

FEB. 3. An horrendous few weeks, in every regard; first this dire weather, which began when? It was an ordinary winter until Harris vanished, as if he took with him what benevolence the season might vouchsafe to offer; thus we sit girdled in a dark and wrathful freeze. The poet knows—

. . . cruelest Winter's iron jaws
lock down so tight the tendons sing . . .

How many of our neighbors are done in by this storm? Desperate Burger and his skinny boy thresh up, hauling themselves over one mountainous drift after another all the way from Yorby, seeking forty lost head of beef; their trek fruitless. . . . And I learn today from our good Sheriff Pfeiffer—who comes sliding up on what can only be called a royal toboggan—that Burger's stock was all jammed into a fence corner on his own land, the lot visible from the roof of his own house, had the snow been six feet less.

We have more to be thankful for than does Burger; as Otto and the boys, yeomen all, by hand drag armloads of hay across the drifts where our cattle flounder; and chop free those fastened to the ice by the heat of their muzzles. A loss, of course, but a negligible one, next to the disasters around us; and at the first hint of a thaw, we will retrieve those dozens gone, for their hides, and whatever frozen parts are still good for the table or other use— this last a circumspect business: not everyone believes frozen beef is good beef. . . .

So brief is the Sheriff's visit that I wonder why he bothers: he has only a single question: What word is there from Harris? We know our duty to report such, do we not?

Emil, say I. There is nothing here but storm upon storm. In two weeks, before you, I have seen only one man.

Not as if to pry, says Pfeiffer, but who would that be?

Burger, say I, and so I learn of Burger's discovery so close to his own home—and also of another catastrophe: the little Erickson girl. Her teacher, hoping to fetch the little girl home at noon, in the worst of it, got no farther than Gantz's place—not that it is visible in the solid white surrounding; but in his haystack, the teacher burrowed a cave. It was not enough.

No way to keep the little girl warm, said Emil. Froze her own feet off too, looks like.

Erickson's little girl? say I. Damn the luck of that! I saw her once or twice—pretty white hair, all curls. . . . Damn. . . . We will send something over there.

Yes, yes, says Emil. That would be good. They are in terrible shape over there. And others too, Goddamn it!.... But listen, Gerhardt, you would tell me if you heard from Harris, eh?

Emil, say I with force, I have heard nothing but the damn blasted wind, and I have had enough of that; and now you add to it.

Emil waves his hand. It will get better, he says.

You tell me when, say I; and sign your name to it; but he is gone off on his fancy toboggan in a cloud of steam from his overheated pony.

Otto, who is always listening, says: Well, *there* is Beidermann's hay; let him buy up what Burger does not need anymore.

THE TWINS ARE in a fit of concern, with something only now discovered: the little Jersey, a pet of the two for her soulful eyes, and tended and milked only by them—they drank her warm milk—half-cream, it seemed, unless Otto or one of the other boys saw them at it—having sought out the lea of the barn in the storm, enough out of it so her warm bag melted the snow it touched; and when the temperature plummeted in an hour to turn the world into ice, well there she was caught, cruelly tethered to the ice by her frozen udder. The twins chopped her free; but no matter. At supper, Otto looks at me over the ham hocks and string beans and shakes his head:She's a goner, he says. So the damage has been done; she will not be milked again, should she live.

FEB. 5. So cold it is that we scarcely leave the house, except to bring in stalks and hay twists to feed our pale fire. . . .

Ma has solved her annual problem of where to store her sauerkraut crocks—the root cellar, although having room, being too cold—by having the twins haul the huge jugs up the stairs to the bedroom of Henry, Cornelius, and Harris, there being space under the window on Harris' side; and for all they appreciate a spicy hank of the vegetable on their supper plates, Cornelius and Henry look askance at the three big crocks, for they do produce a scent, and take up more room than Harris.

We will move them out, says Ma, once Harris is back.

So that ends their grumbling; and now, to accompany their snores, they have the frequent plop of a gaseous bubble, from under the window.

FEB. 6. Rain follows the plow, the pretty little catalogues from the railroad have trumpeted for years now: indeed, it is almost biblical: *Yea, Rain doth Follow the Plow.* And behind that promise from the Eastern companies come the greenhorns; who flock in still, holding out their cups for a drink of rain. And go dry; as one old boy white-washed letters on the side of his wagon as he headed east: *Bust in Dakota, No Rain.*

But there is something that follows the plow—and that is *snow.* It follows not only the plow but most everything; for sure, it follows the Praeger family. Where we look is all snow. In some winters paths blow open across stubbly fields, where a man could almost stroll in his slippers; but not this winter: even Gulliver in hip boots could not easily cross these brutal drifts. The prudent man stays in his house. . . .

And yet, through and across, into and out of, up and over the corrugations of this barren landscape, there thresh the twins; they haul their last load of our hay to their friend and mentor; and the horses pitch into the drifts at their shouts.

Shaking his head, Otto watches them plow off. If they hurt that team . . . he says; and walks to the barn, kicking gouts of snow out of his way in the head-high chute the boys shovel daily to keep clear, against the wind.

FEB. 8. There is less to say, surely less to set down here; and less to say aloud for us all. At breakfast, dinner, supper, it is mostly silence; perhaps as we speak less we think less too, having shut out painful ideas. . . .

Harris: his name goes unspoken; but perhaps conveyed in a way of looking—certainly from Ma. Beidermann too, another name unspoken, but for the twins, and they have a code.

Thus we push through the confinement of each cold day, with essential matters gone unuttered. It is not impossible to do this: it is easier, for it provides a queer tranquility, which fastens to the season, as the poet knows:

. . . the silences of winter.

FEB. 10. I look at what last I wrote: yes, the silences—indeed, the hush—of winter. The hush in this household, a moldering hush: a dire hush laid upon the human hearts of an old man and his family who must answer for a truant dog-poisoner and barn-burner. No one can say it aloud, and we are sorrowfully limited now in what we say and to whom we say it. Can we talk to Beidermann, then? Or do we bid for membership in that confraternity of our neighbors who live their lives as they regard each other in mutual and contemptuous silence? Many here have got themselves into that fix: the Bells and Gruntvigs; the Placertons and Peckners; and famously the Foss and Gustavson families—not a word spoken between them for two decades, the early disagreement forgotten—and we have one of the Foss boys marry the oldest Gustavson girl; they move to Montana,promptly; with those left behind maintaining full silence. . . . On an afternoon, a year or two back, our business done, I talk with Schwantz in the doorway of his store; and he pokes my shoulder, pointing up the road and saying: Watch this now.

It is old man Foss approaching from the east; and then Schwantz motions down the road: old man Gustavson strides at us from the same side.

Now, says Schwantz, as pleased as if this is a display he has been at pains to arrange: watch this fancy footwork; as the two men, each taking note of the other at the same time, haul up sharply; and Foss, quickest of the two, makes a neat two-step across the road as if that was his intention all along, for all that only a vacancy of weeds and sunflowers awaited him.

Schwantz chuckled. Hey, he says, better than if they are shooting at each other, eh?

And now I unhappily foresee years of the Praegers and Mister Beidermann and his progeny, should any occur, fancily side-stepping each other on the icy byways of Skiles . . .

FEB. 13. It approaches midnight; and having fed the last handy twist of straw to the kitchen stove, and having studied the dying coals through the crack of the door, I will pause at this ledger, and perhaps more than pause. How long can we live this frigid life, each day more icily daunting than the one before? It takes all heart from a man, this bleak and harsh season. . . . What follows the plow? Snow follows the plow, and follows . . . and follows . . . and follows. . . .

What is there to write, then? The cold causes the pen to slip, my fingers little warmed for being tucked into my armpits, however well that strategy suits the twins, whose mittens sprout holes as fast as Ma darns them over. . . .

Yet into this piercing air comes a moth, a ragged, worn-out creature in a foredoomed struggle around my lamp chimney, where it knocks itself dizzy in a frenzy to what?—escape Ma's cedar chips? To find a passage to more benign territory? But it bangs around, losing dust from its tattered wings, hastening its end.

I NTER-LEAF

IT WAS SOMETHING BLACK up ahead, a half-mile off, along that snow-covered incline running north off the old freight road along which Corporal Doggett and his detail plowed their way. Hard to tell what; maybe it wasn't even alive; it didn't move. Near it was a big rock, almost buried in snow.

"Hey," Doggett yelled back to the kid on the horse behind him, who was wrapped in a blanket to make a hood over his head, out of which came the steam of his breath. He looked not at all soldierly, and indeed, out of the four rug-and-blanket enfolded privates who trailed the Corporal, Doggett alone, with his upright bearing and official great-coat—and the three pack mules with *U.S. Army* branded on their rears—betrayed the military nature of the group.

Behind Doggett, the boy bent over with sneezing and when he recovered, he looked bleary-eyed from under his blanket hood. "Huh?"

Doggett pointed. "What the hell is that over there?"

The boy pushed back his hood and wiped a mitten across his watery eyes, and saw nothing more than a continuing landscape of snow, hardly differing from anything he had seen since leaving Snelling three days ago. Then he saw the big rock.

"'At's a rock," he said.

"Aw, Gawd," said the Corporal. "Down off to the bottom there. What's that? Is that a horse?"

Coughing, the boy squinted long and hard. "Well, it might be."

Doggett knew his soldierly obligations. "You go on and see what that's all about. If it gets late we'll wait on you at the crick. Get a move on."

The boy's horse was big, a five-year-old roan gelding that had stepped along easily on the blown-over freight road and had only slightly more trouble heading through the deeper snow toward the big rock.

What had pricked the Corporal's interest was indeed a horse— an almost dead horse, the boy saw, which hardly moved its head at their noisy approach through chest-deep snow. It was a shabby old bay gelding, its cinch partly torn so the saddle hung under its belly, anchored in the snow. Its head hung without moving, the warmth of its nose having melted a small depression in the snow to accommodate its breathing.

"You poor bastard," said the boy. He unwrapped himself, wiped his nose on his sleeve, and lowered himself into the drift. With his knife he finished the tear in the cinch and pulled the saddle free. He punched some of the snow off. It wasn't worth a nickel; just rotten-looking wood in the frame, the leather scraped off or hanging in fringes.

But as he threw the saddle aside, the boy found something else attached to a short piece of rope on the pommel—an old rifle. From muzzle to stock, snow and ice had attached itself to the firearm, and he couldn't tell if it was worth anything. He knocked most of the snow off and strung the rope on his own saddle, wondering whether this find was something the Corporal needed to know about.

The old bay hadn't moved. This was one sick horse, thought the boy. Why in hell was it out here in the middle of nowhere, not a tree or anything in sight? Who owned this horse, the saddle, the rifle? He sure as hell was a goner, thought the boy . . . out here.

He wiped his nose on his mitten and looked toward the road where the detail moved along slowly, back toward Fort Buford— they'd be there tomorrow night, if another Goddamned storm didn't decide to come in and freeze everybody's asses off. He climbed into his blankets on the roan, the horse anxious to get back to his pals moving away from him on the road.

Looking back, the boy saw the old bay make its first real move, raising its head as if to watch his departure.

Poor bastard sure could use something to eat, the boy thought. There was plenty of oats and a little corn in the mule packs, but he wasn't going to ride down to get it. Then he remembered the stale bread in his saddlebag. A fellow never knew when he might want a little extra. The army usually gave you enough to eat, but a lot of it was crap you didn't want, not even as good as yesterday's leftovers. Lots of stuff he had saved that he didn't end up eating, but the dogs and chickens and the ornery hog at the fort sure loved it.

Out of the bag he dug a large handful of crusty bread, five or six big slices, and leaned over with it to the old bay. He wasn't a foot from its nose before the whole lot disappeared—just sucked it up, just like that.

Jeez, the boy thought, I coulda lost a hand there! The horse watched for more.

"You're gonna have to come and get it yourself, my friend," said the boy, and set off to retrace his trail to the freight road, where the detail's caboose mule was just visible a mile ahead. Behind, the old bay nag came along, steadily.

Smells them oats, thought the boy.